De

Reguiba.

Tall and thin, with the aquiline features and weathered skin of the desert-born, Reguiba was dressed all in black, deliberate in his movements. Ominous. Sinister. Holstered on both hips were twin Colt .45s.

"Had you the wit to slay the spy along with Lemniak, I might have let you live," Reguiba said to the agents. "As it is . . . "

He did not complete the sentence, nor did he need to. Not all his men spoke English, but all knew when their master had decreed death . . .

The agents were hanged face to face on the same rope. Reguiba pulled a hawking glove on his right hand, and whistled. His falcon fluttered down from the roof beams, alighting on his outstretched arm. He stroked the bird's head while watching the fun . . .

NICK CARTER IS IT!

FROM THE NICK CARTER
KILLMASTER SERIES

NICK CARTER

KILLMASTER

Blood Of The Falcon

CHARTER BOOKS, NEW YORK

BLOOD OF THE FALCON

A Charter Book/published by arrangement with
The Condé Nast Publications, Inc.

PRINTING HISTORY
Charter edition/February 1987

ISBN: 0-441-57291-X

Charter Books are published by The Berkley Publishing Group,
200 Madison Avenue, New York, New York 10016.
PRINTED IN THE UNITED STATES OF AMERICA

*Dedicated to the men and women of the
Secret Service of the
United States of America*

ONE

One hot morning in early June, the *Melina* rode at anchor a mile out from the Israeli coast. The freighter was a floating bomb manned by a crew of killers.

The prospect of getting off the ship failed to cheer veteran terrorist Bassam Abu-Bakir. The only way to leave was by boat, and the thirty-two-year-old Palestinian, a born landlubber, loathed all things nautical. Throughout this trip he'd suffered from seasickness. Even now, he felt poorly.

Soon he'd feel worse. Much worse.

Hasim teased him. "Abu-Bakir, why so glum? The great day is here at last. Your heart should rejoice in gladness!"

"My heart will rejoice when it's safely back on dry land, and not before. *Inshallah*," Abu-Bakir added, "if God wills it."

Hasim nodded. "Our fate rests in the hands of Allah. If we are destined to die at sea, so be it. If not, then nothing can harm us. In any case, whatever is written shall come to pass."

"What a comfort you are." Abu-Bakir spat over the rail, into the sea.

Young Hasim was classified as a demolitions "expert." That meant only that he could rig a simple bomb without blowing himself up.

The *Melina* could blow without help from Hasim or anybody else. Stored in the central cargo hold were four tons of C-4–type plastique explosives bought in Cyprus at a bargain price. Too late, the load was found to be dangerously unstable. Since then, most of the crew lived in fear that some slight jarring impact would trigger a chain reaction in the cargo, blasting the ship to kingdom come.

The situation didn't bother Hasim at all. A Lebanese Shiite, he was there on loan from his local branch of the Islamic Jihad group. Compared to his home turf in the shooting gallery of the Bekaa Valley, this sea voyage was a pleasure cruise.

Being somewhat of a joker, Hasim enjoyed needling the dour Abu-Bakir. He nudged the Palestinian. "Hey, here comes your pal, Solano!"

Abu-Bakir bristled. "What? Where—?"

Following Hasim's gaze, Abu-Bakir set eyes on Solano, a man he very much wanted dead. His face darkened and his scowl deepened.

Hasim went on, "How fortunate that you two are together in the same squad! You're such good friends, I know you couldn't bear to be parted."

Abu-Bakir was totally unamused.

"If you and the Italian fight the enemy half as hard as you fight each other, the Zionists will be pushed into the sea in no time."

"Had I the time, Hasim, I would show you what I think of your humor."

Hasim giggled.

Solano and Vernex approached the ready area at the rail, hand-carrying their meager personal gear.

Pierre-Michel Vernex was once a graduate student and still looked the part. A pallid Swiss, he had carroty hair, turnip-colored flesh, and a pear-shaped body. In times past, he deconstructed philosophical tracts with scholarly logic. Now he deconstructed capitalist society with the tools of terror.

A string of successful bank robberies and abductions of high-ranking NATO personnel marked Giacomo Solano as a fast-rising star of the political underworld. High risk for high pay was his formula for the good life. Gifted with a cruelly handsome face and fine physique, he seemed more playboy than master criminal.

Anarchist, bomber, assassin—whatever else he might be, it was clear that Solano was a bit of a dandy. As always, his sleek black hair was carefully brushed back, his beard neatly trimmed. He wore a jaunty yachting cap, navy blue nylon windbreaker, white open-neck shirt, beige chino pants, and deck shoes with no socks.

Vernex snorted. "You look like a bourgeois banker set for a day of boating."

"Just because this is an ugly business, it doesn't mean I have to dress ugly," Solano said.

Earlier in the voyage, Abu-Bakir sneered at Solano for what he considered an unmanly concern with neatness and good grooming, and even openly referred to him as "the powderpuff." His derision lasted right up to the Great Dolphin Massacre and its aftermath, following which his contempt was transformed to hot, raw hatred.

No one knew what prodigious self-control it now took Abu-Bakir to turn his back on the newcomers and deliberately ignore them.

Solano was not so easily put off. "Good morning, Hasim."

Hasim smiled, nodded.

"And a very good morning to you, Abu-Bakir."

The Palestinian responded by grinding his bad teeth in impotent rage.

Solano put down his bag, stretched, went to the rail,

and swallowed a few lungfuls of fresh air. "Ah, that's good! What a pleasure it will be to finally get off this stinking tub of a ship! I'm sure you agree, Abu-Bakir. Not too talkative today, are you? What's the matter, my friend? Cat got your tongue?"

Solano pretended to study the sprawling blue seascape. "Hmmmm, I don't see any dolphins today . . ."

That did it. Unsure of the Palestinian's reaction to the taunt, a no-longer-grinning Hasim joined Vernex in moving quickly to the side, out of the potential line of fire.

Self-restraint didn't wear well on Abu-Bakir. His face twitched. His hands shook from the struggle of stifling his murderous urges.

Trembling with tight-lipped rage, Abu-Bakir stalked off, Hasim trailing him by a few paces.

Vernex let out the breath he'd been holding. "You live dangerously, Solano."

Solano's broad grin flashed dazzling white teeth in a deeply tanned face. "Our comrade in arms doesn't like me so well, eh?"

"You are very stupid to provoke him."

"I caught the bastard machine-gunning dolphins for target practice, so I knocked him down. What of it?"

"You took his gun away from him and threatened to use it on him if he did it again," Vernex reminded the Italian.

"That was a promise, not a threat. Besides, Abu-Bakir is an extremist. Subtlety is wasted on him," Solano said. "Anyway, I like dolphins. Such beautiful creatures! You know, it's bad luck to kill them."

"It's worse luck to cross Abu-Bakir. He'd as soon kill you as look at you."

"So why doesn't he try?"

"The only thing that stops him from shooting you is that a stray slug could set off the explosives."

"The only thing? I wonder . . ."

"Once we're off the ship—beware," Vernex warned.

"I can take care of myself. But I thank you for the concern."

"I'm concerned with anything that might adversely affect our mission."

"You're a dedicated man, Vernex."

"True. Dedicated to the cause of world socialist revolution."

"Me, I'm dedicated to the holy cause of Solano."

"Your cynicism is disgusting," Vernex muttered.

"But my shooting is first rate," Solano said. "That's why I'm here."

Along came the hulking man-mountain known only as "Elias." "Ah, there you are! I have been looking for you guys."

Elias resembled nothing so much as a bear waddling on its hind legs. An apt comparison, since a single swipe from either of his big, clumsy hands could cave in a man's face or smash his skull. He belonged to ETA-Militar, the ultraviolent Basque separatist army. He was a long way from his mountain home in the Pyrenees, but terror makes strange bedfellows. When told by his commanders that he was being loaned out to their comrades in the international terrorist network, Elias obeyed without a murmur.

Elias, Abu-Bakir, Solano, Vernex. The four members of the operation's Rocket Attack Squad.

"Our boat's loaded," Elias said. "Time to go." He looked around for the missing team member. "Where's Abu-Bakir?"

Abu-Bakir angrily stalked the ways of the ship's superstructure. He ran into Driss, the slave of Mokhtar. The collision sent Driss sprawling.

"Fool!" Abu-Bakir barked. "Why don't you watch where you're going!" Fighting the urge to strike the smaller man, he strode away.

Nimble Driss hopped up from the deck plates, chased Abu-Bakir, caught and held him the the sleeve. "He wants you."

"Who?"

Driss snorted. "You know who."

Abu-Bakir knew who, all right, but he was in no mood to be trifled with, not even by the operation's leader. "Tell your master I'm too busy to chat. I have to go blow up a Zionist oil dump."

"You think he doesn't know that?" Driss let go of Abu-Bakir's sleeve. Without another word, he turned and walked away.

After a pause for second thoughts, Abu-Bakir raced after him. "Wait! Where are you going?"

"To tell Mokhtar you refuse his summons."

"Don't be so hasty. Of course I will see him. Where is he?"

"Follow me," the slave commanded.

Abu-Bakir obeyed. Driss led him up a steep metal stairway into the ship's upper works, along a starboard gangway, around a corner, through a dark corridor, around another corner into blinding daylight, down a narrow aisle, around yet another blind corner, and into an alcove roofed over by a green-striped deck awning.

There stood Mokhtar, sudden, unexpected. Abu-Bakir stopped short to keep from stumbling into the man.

Mokhtar made a sign to his slave. Driss vanished.

Mokhtar was balding, wide-faced, with a black mustache and goatee. His age was indeterminate. He could have been a dissipated forty or a vigorous sixty. He wore a rumpled brown pin-striped Western business suit and brown wing-tip shoes. A long-sleeved gray shirt was buttoned up to the collar. He wore no tie.

Stuffed butt-forward in the top of his trousers was a revolver, a Spanish copy of a Smith & Wesson .38. He preferred a rifle, with which he was a championship marksman, but handguns were a necessary evil. Especially when working in close quarters, as for example on board the *Melina*.

Knives were necessary too. He wore a flat-bladed throwing knife sheathed between his shoulder blades, out of sight but within easy reach.

Immune to the midday heat, his taut flesh was dry as dust. So was his voice as he said, "You recall our little talk, Abu-Bakir?"

"Yes."

Abu-Bakir recalled it all too well. The dolphin incident occurred on the first day out from port, before the volatile cargo put an end to shipboard horseplay. During the fracas, Solano got his hands on Abu-Bakir's AK-47, his trusty Kalashnikov automatic rifle. Before returning it, Solano removed the weapon's magazine and tossed it overboard.

Mokhtar had intercepted the Palestinian while he was hunting high and low for a loaded clip to empty into Solano. "The Italian is needed for now. Do him harm, and you must answer to my master."

"I answer to no man!" Abu-Bakir had declared. "My master is Allah alone!"

"My master is Reguiba."

That had unnerved Abu-Bakir. "R-Reguiba?"

Mokhtar had permitted himself a thin smile at the other's evident distress. "You know that name—Reguiba? You have heard of the man who bears that name?"

"I—yes. I have heard of him."

"Then a word to the wise will suffice. And that word is *Reguiba*," Mokhtar had concluded, dismissing him.

Abu-Bakir had heard and obeyed. That was the sole reason why Solano was still alive.

But now, under the green-striped awning, Mokhtar took a different tack. "We must have another little talk. I have given much thought to a certain matter."

"Yes?"

"When your mission is done—and *only* then—it would be well if the man Solano was no more."

Abu-Bakir was cautious. "This is Reguiba's wish?"

"Reguiba does not concern himself with such trifles. He demands only that your raid succeed. This is my wish. And, no doubt, your fond desire."

"To be sure." Exulting, Abu-Bakir nodded his head rapidly. "A thousand thanks, Mokhtar!" An idea struck him. "And what of the other two unbelievers, the giant and the Swiss?"

"What of them? As you say, they are only unbelievers. Do what you will, but I remind you that one can escape the hunters more easily than three. Is that not so?"

"Indeed!"

Mokhtar raised a hand in ritual benediction. "Now go forth and kill, Bassam Abu-Bakir! And may the blessings of the Prophet be upon you."

"As you command." Abu-Bakir salaamed as he withdrew from Mokhtar's presence, visions of murder dancing brightly in his head.

TWO

The accommodation ladder stood at the ship's star-board quarter. Specially installed for the mission, its bright yellow metal scaffolding contrasted with the black, rusted hull like a brand-new fire escape slapped on a condemned building. At its base bobbed a floating platform dock. Moored to the dock were twin power-boats, sleekly streamlined high-performance jobs.

The boats had made the trip riding piggyback on the ship. When the *Melina* dropped anchor off Tel Aviv, they were hoisted out of their afterdeck berths and lowered into the sea, a nerve-racking job for crane operator and crew alike, considering the cargo's vulner-ability to sudden shocks.

Now the boats were in the water, ready to go. One was reserved for the Rocket Attack Squad. The other was the getaway boat, slated for use when the crew abandoned ship. It didn't take a genius to see that the launch lacked the capacity to carry off all the members of the ship's skeleton crew, but everybody figured that it was the other guy who'd get it in the neck when the time came.

Gorgias, the first mate, bossed a pair of sailors who

did all the work of getting the boats squared away.

When the quartet of rocketeers assembled on the plat-form dock, Gorgias sidled over to them. Casting a twisted glance toward the ship's upper works, he hissed, "What's Captain Farmingdale up to now?"

"The last I saw of him, he was on the bridge, busy minding his own business," Solano replied. "The cap-tain doesn't care to be associated with the likes of us."

"That's good for you. It's not safe to be near him."

"Why not?"

"His bad luck can rub off on you. You are well rid of him. I cannot wait until I am."

Solano chuckled. "Still holding to your pet theory?"

"It's no theory; it's a fact. I know!" Gorgias was a dark, squat, strong man laid low by obsessive fear. Fear not of the cargo, but of the captain. The first mate looked ill, with clammy gray flesh and black circles ringing his haunted eyes.

"Ask any sailor who's ever shipped out with him, and they'll tell you the same—the ones who came back to port, that is. Captain Farmingdale is a jinx. A Jonah!"

Insurance companies are well aware of the phenom-enon of persons labeled "accident prones," luckless in-dividuals who through no fault of their own are dogged by catastrophe. Seamen call such persons "Jonahs," af-ter the biblical prophet, the original hard-luck mariner.

A crewman stood at the top of the ladder, shouting down. "Hey, Gorgias! The captain wants to see you!"

Muttering darkly, the first mate threw up his hands in despair—or perhaps resignation—and hurried to the bridge.

Vernex snickered. "Jonahs and jinxes—what utter tripe! Trust a sailor to swallow such imbecilic drivel! Even so, let's be off. Why stay here any longer than necessary?"

The four men clambered aboard one of the boats. A pair of stylish bucket seats faced the control console.

Solano took the wheel and Vernex sat beside him. Elias and Abu-Bakir sat aft, facing one another. Heavy-duty weapons wrapped in waterproof bags were piled between them on the bottom of the boat.

Abu-Bakir enjoyed the strategic advantage of being behind Solano's back. He delighted in having his fully loaded AK-47 slung across his shoulder. But he hated giving up the solidity of the ship for the insecurity of this comparatively tiny craft bobbing on the big blue sea. By steadily staring at his feet and nowhere else, he stabilized his nausea.

Solano fired her up. Twin engines turned over like a dream, purring with smooth power. Needles flipped to their marks on the gauges and dials.

"She's a beauty!" Solano said.

The powerboat's advanced design and curvilinear gullwing hull identified her as a Superbo Mark V, a top-of-the-line vessel not so much built as lovingly hand-crafted by the world-renowned Genoese boatyards of the Agnelli family. She could make the fastest patrol boat look like the proverbial slow boat to China by comparison.

The mooring lines were untied. The boat shoved off, slowly steering clear of the *Melina*.

"Look." Elias pointed out a solitary figure standing at the ship's stern rail, silently seeing them off. "Mokhtar."

Vernex waved to him. His fluttering arm trailed off limply as he realized Mokhtar hadn't the slightest intention of returning the farewell salute.

Vernex shrugged and settled into his seat. "A strange sort of fellow."

Abu-Bakir could not resist a little anticipatory gloating. "He is deep . . . very deep. Deeper than you could ever dream. And his master is deeper still."

"Oh? And who might that be?" Vernex asked. "I think we'd all like to know the identity of the mysterious employer who recruited us for this job."

Had he given away too much? Abu-Bakir wondered. He decided to play it cagey. "Mokhtar's master? Why, none other than God, of course. Allah is the master of all men."

"Deep," Vernex scoffed. "That's very deep."

Steering one-handed, Solano rapped the boat box bolted to the floorboard. "What's inside?"

Vernex flipped open the lid and rummaged through the gear. "Charts . . . floats . . . flare pistol . . . line . . . first-aid kit . . . everything one needs for a sea cruise. Our boss is very thorough."

"Whoever he is," Solano said.

"My boss is the People, the masses."

"Yes, yes, anything you say."

The Superbo emerged from the ship's shadow into the dazzling fullness of the noonday sun. Solano slipped on a pair of polarized Porsche sunglasses. He opened up the throttle. The boat zoomed south.

Vernex shouted to be heard over the roaring twin inboard engines. "I don't mind telling you, I'm glad to be off the ship!"

Abu-Bakir seized on this. "You were afraid."

"Of the ship blowing up? Certainly!"

"Hah! I was not afraid." Grinning, Abu-Bakir sat back with an air of superiority, as if he had one-upped Vernex for all time.

Aft, the *Melina* dwindled in the north. West, the open sea stretched to the curved horizon. To the east lay Tel Aviv's urban sprawl, modern buildings sprouting like crystals from the rocks of that ancient land. The present gave way to the past as the old port city of Jaffa swung into view in the south.

Less than a quarter-hour's forward hurtling motion brought them within reach of their target.

Some miles north of Ashkelon and Ashdod, the shoreline curved outward into the sea, forming a cape.

On its tip sat the Shamash petroleum complex, a newly built oil depot containing storage and refining facilities.

The rocketeers' target.

Silence fell as Solano cut the motors, idling the boat far enough out to avoid attracting the attention of the curious.

In the distance, numerous small craft sailed about the man-made harbor. Berthed at the site's quarter-mile-long piers were two transatlantic supertankers unloading their precious cargo. Precious indeed for a nation that imports 100 percent of its fuel.

The massive main complex rose above the harbor like an enchanted city. Huge silvery cylinders and spheres bore the bold blue-and-white sunburst logo of the state-owned Shamash company. These storage tanks were threaded with a delicate web of catwalks, pipes, and support struts. It was a scene of bustling activity.

Vernex licked his lips and broke the silence. "A duck shoot."

"Easier," Solano said. "Ducks don't sit still, waiting for you to blow them away."

"Let's not keep them waiting."

"Break out the launchers!" Elias rumbled.

"Yes, by all means." Vernex made his way aft, where the weapons waited. They were bagged rather than crated to minimize weight, maximizing boat speed.

In effect, the Superbo was a seagoing rocket-launching platform. The rocketeers would zip into the harbor, destroy the complex and any other convenient targets—such as the tanker ships—then race to the rendezvous point.

Vernex, Elias, and Abu-Bakir tore at the fastenings of the bright orange nylon bags. The unveiling of the weapons caught them up in a primal quickening, a kind of sexually intense trance. In the thrill of the moment, Abu-Bakir even forgot his queasiness, though not his intended double cross.

Except that Solano got there first.

"Hey!" Solano said it two more times, loudly, before the others looked up. When they did, they saw the gun in his hand.

It was a chunky, squarish, Soviet-made Tokarev TT-33 pistol, and it was pointing at them.

At that moment, their nausea had nothing to do with seasickness.

Only the gentle swell, slapping the hull, broke the intense stillness.

Finally Vernex said, "What's this, Solano?"

"The end of the line."

Vernex's forced smile crumbled at the edges. "We have much to do, so please don't joke."

He was faking. He knew it was no joke. His eyes narrowed as he calculated his chances. He couldn't believe that he was on the wrong side of a gun.

"Traitor!" Abu-Bakir cried.

"Spy, actually," Solano said. "The party's over, boys."

Solano was over too. In that instant, he ceased to exist. He had never really existed at all, despite the evidence to the contrary. Because "Giacomo Solano" was a man who never was. His was an artificially constructed identity, a "legend" in the jargon of the trade. The trade being espionage, specifically espionage of the AXE variety.

AXE was the ultrasecret action component of the U.S. intelligence community. One of the last real secrets left in an open, democratic society, and quite possibly that society's last bullwark against global anarchy.

The AXE agent who was "Solano" now took off that identity like a suit of clothes. His name, his *real* name, was Nick Carter.

Code-named N3, Carter was AXE's top Killmaster.

THREE

Elias raged.

A fatalist, he knew that someday his number would come up, just as he knew he'd never go to prison, never be taken alive. When he thought about his own death, he always fancied that he'd go out in a blaze of glory, taking along a gang of policemen to keep him company in Hell.

Who was this absurd Judas, this treacherous insect threatening him with his ridiculous popgun? Such arrogance was insulting, not to be borne.

"A spy! A goddamned spy!" This development struck Abu-Bakir as so funny that he burst into hysterical laughter.

Roaring, Elias rushed Carter.

The Killmaster didn't waste words. He snapped off two shots into Elias, both hits scoring in the torso. But when a body that big gets moving, it's hard to stop.

Carter tried to sidestep the Basque's headlong rush, but the cramped forward compartment left him little room in which to maneuver. Elias crashed into him, taking him down.

Carter fell hard, shoulders slamming into the boat

15

box with stunning impact. His pistol slapped up against the hull with a wicked smack, but somehow he kept hold of it.

Elias wallowed on top of Carter, crushing the breath out of him. Huge hands sought the agent's throat, found it, squeezed.

The power of that crushing grip was awesome. If Elias hadn't been weakened from taking two bullets in the belly, he'd have wrung Carter's neck as if it were a chicken's.

"Kill him! Kill him!"

Vernex clawed a pistol out of his pocket and started shooting. He was fast, but not accurate. Three shots exploded: one passed harmlessly out to sea, and the other two missed Carter, hitting Elias.

The Basque convulsed under the penetrating impact of the slugs. He gave Carter's neck a final choking squeeze, then went limp.

Shaking himself out of his hysteria, Abu-Bakir unslung his automatic rifle. Rage and fear sparked his urge to kill.

"No!" Vernex knew what would happen if Abu-Bakir cut loose with a burst of AK-47 rounds: they'd rip right through the spy, smashing the controls, perforating the bottom of the boat.

His free hand waved in frantic warning. "Don't! You'll sink us!"

But Abu-Bakir was beyond recall. He flipped the selector to autofire, as Vernex feared he would. He reached for the trigger just as Vernex shot him.

Fired point-blank, the slug tore into the astonished Palestinian with a meaty thud, taking him in the side.

Abu-Bakir lurched, groaning. He was swinging his rifle muzzle around when Vernex shot him twice more, crying, "Die, die!"

"No, *you* die!" Abu-Bakir whipped the gun around until it pointed at Vernex.

Vernex's scream was obliterated by roaring rapid-fire rounds. He was obliterated along with his scream, being cut almost in half by the sustained blast.

His dead weight thumped into the bottom of the boat.

A heartbeat later he was joined by Abu-Bakir. Hunched forward on his knees, the terrorist dropped his weapon and held his shattered chest.

Blood covered his hands, dripping through his fingers. Red foam bubbled out of his moaning mouth.

It all went down in just a very few seconds.

Nick Carter wasn't one to look a gift horse in the mouth. He squirmed, working his upper body free from Elias until he was sitting up. His pistol drew a bead on Abu-Bakir's bowed head. He pulled the trigger, to deliver the coup de grâce.

Nothing happened.

The Tokarev must have jammed when he took that hard fall.

Hot light flickered behind the film of Abu-Bakir's fast-dulling eyes. He sized up the situation at a glance.

Carter worked the slide, futilely trying to free the pistol's action.

"Ahhhh . . . having problems, spy?" Chuckling, Abu-Bakir picked up his rifle. He stopped chuckling as he coughed up some blood, but he kept on smiling.

Even a jammed gun is good for something. Carter threw it at Abu-Bakir. It bounced harmlessly off the Palestinian's shoulder, but Carter made good use of the split-second diversion it provided.

The Killmaster flipped open the boat box lid, grabbed the flare gun, and fired. A miniature sun erupted from the muzzle, exploding square in the middle of Abu-Bakir's grinning face.

The Palestinian jumped up screaming, his scorched flesh bubbling. His face was a charred, smoking piece of meat. Arms flailing, beard and hair burning, face melting, he careened off the sides of the boat.

He hit the port gunwale too hard and flipped overboard. A big splash marked where he fell into the sea. His gear weighed him down, and he swiftly sank from sight.

Nick Carter dragged his legs out from under Elias and climbed into the seat behind the wheel. He sprawled there, recovering, taking stock of his injuries.

His throat ached from the Basque's death grip. He could hardly swallow. Where he hit the boat box, his upper back felt like one big bruise. His ribs were tender but uncracked. He was stiff, shaky, and sore, but nothing was broken.

He was lucky to have gotten off so lightly. Especially after doing something so stupid.

He should have shot down all three without warning, but he wanted to see the look on their faces when they discovered that their mission had gone sour. That little personal indulgence nearly cost Carter his own life. He vowed not to let his emotions interfere with the job at hand.

High overhead, a silver jet slashed a chalky white contrail across the remote blue dome of the sky. The sun blazed. Carter mentally pictured Tel Aviv's golden beaches, jammed with fun-seekers on this gorgeous day.

And any moment now, the *Melina* would make its final run, might already be making it, even now—

Time to get moving.

Carter shook his head to clear it, fighting dizziness. He pushed back hair that had fallen across his face, brushing it back with his fingers. His hands were steady enough.

Groaning, he stumbled aft, picking his way over Elias and Vernex. He saw no sign of Abu-Bakir, not so much as a ripple or a bubble. Too bad. The Abu Nidal faction of the Palestinian Liberation Front would just have to get along without him.

He picked up the Tokarev and shook his head. Even

the Soviets had phased it out in favor of the Makarov
SL. That was what he got for going into the field minus
Wilhelmina, his lethal Luger. But he had been under the
deepest cover and couldn't risk being recognized as the
formidable AXE operative who had terminated so many
top enemy agents with a 9mm Luger.

It was an anxious moment when the Tokarev jammed,
but Carter wasn't entirely without resources. If the flare
gun hadn't been at hand, he still would have had an ace
up his sleeve—quite literally. He hadn't left all his old
friends at home.

He tossed the pistol into the sea. Time to bring out the
big guns. Luckily, he had a boat full of them.

It was also full of blood. Vernex's corpse sprawled
across the weapons. Abu-Bakir's sustained blast had
chopped Vernex through the middle. When Carter
hefted the dead man, Vernex's upper half came apart
from his lower half.

Fighting hard to keep down the contents of his
stomach, Carter heaved both halves overboard. The fish
would feed well today.

Elias could stay where he was for a while. Carter
didn't have the time or strength to wrestle that huge
hulk over the side.

He hauled two fairly dry weapons bags forward, putting them on the passenger seat. Opening one, he took
out a rocket launcher.

A portable shoulder-fired job, its smoothbore firing
tube was a three-foot-long piece of olive-drab plastic
pipe as thick around as a man's arm. Protective cover-
ings sealed its ends, while the sighting and trigger mechanisms were folded down flat.

Carter unbagged the other launcher, securing both
within easy reach. He found his sunglasses under the
control console, intact, unbroken. Donning them, he
glanced at the Shamash complex. It, too, was intact and
unbroken.

Might as well do it up in style, Carter thought. He put on his yachting cap, tilting it to a jaunty angle.

He spun the Superbo around, reversing her so her bow aimed north, then opened the throttle wide. The powerboat took off like a bullet.

The *Melina*'s distant outline was in sight when Carter discovered he was not alone.

A flutter of sliding shadow, a sobbed grunt, a rustle of whispering motion more sensed than heard over the throbbing motors—

Carter was slammed by what felt like a ton of bricks.

Elias wasn't dead. A hard man to kill, the mortally wounded Basque had played possum, gathering what remained of his once great strength to make one last try.

Rising up behind the Killmaster, Elias wrapped his arms around Carter's neck and did his best to break it.

He applied a choke hold. Working from behind gave him advantages in weight and leverage that were only partly offset by his weakness. At full strength, Elias could have effortlessly snapped Carter's spine.

Carter released the wheel. The Superbo streaked forward at full tilt. Carter grabbed the hairy forearm that labored to crush his larynx. He snuggled his chin down to stall the attempt.

The boat was out of control. Swaying, fishtailing, she heeled precariously from side to side.

Elias's head loomed over Carter's right shoulder. He grunted, gasped, but said nothing. His breath smelled like a lion's, hot, foul, blood-scented.

Carter couldn't break the hold before Elias broke his neck, so he stopped trying. Instead, the fingers of his right hand closed on Hugo.

Hugo, the precision-forged stiletto in a chamois sheath strapped to the inside of the Killmaster's right forearm. Hugo, an old and dear friend, was the ace up his sleeve.

Roaring boomed in his ears. Darkness clouded his vision, a darkness that deepened with every second the choke hold cut off oxygen to his brain. Colored lights danced in front of his bulging eyes, sparkling rainbow dots on a field of black.

Strangulation wasn't quick enough to suit Elias. He forced Carter's head backward so he could break his neck across the back of the seat.

A twitch of Carter's arm muscles had tripped Hugo's spring-loaded sheath, popping the hilt into his hand. He stabbed up and back over his shoulder, as hard as he could, so hard that his arm tingled up to the elbow from the force of the blow.

There was a hideous crunching sound as the stiletto thrust into the Basque's forehead, penetrating the skull to lodge deep in the brain. Death was instantaneous.

Elias toppled like a poleaxed steer.

Carter grabbed the wheel, bringing the boat back under control. After slowing its speed to a knot or two, he checked to make sure that Elias was really dead this time.

Indeed he was. But he could still render an important service to the Killmaster.

FOUR

Captain Farmingdale was well aware of his unsavory reputation among seafaring men. That "Jonah" label, hanging around his neck like an albatross, was bosh and nonsense, and damned unfair, too. Every mariner had his share of mishaps during the course of a life spent at sea. Why single out poor old Farmingdale for abuse?

Yes, he'd admit to his share of mishaps and more, but none were really his fault. Any captain might have run one of Her Majesty's naval gunboats around on a sand-bar in the Yangtze River, precipitating an international crisis. The incident of the oil tanker that broke up on the rocks off Brittany—befouling the French coast with a mile-wide spill—he blamed on shoddy navigational equipment and criminally inefficient subordinates.

More recently, he commanded a ship ferrying pil-grims across the Red Sea to Mecca. Shunning age-old tradition, when the boat foundered during a squall, he and the crew saved themselves in the only lifeboats while the passengers went down with the ship. Whose fault was that? The ship's owner, for not supplying enough lifeboats? God's, for sending the storm?

The disaster made him persona non grata in those waters, but it had the happy effect of bringing him to the attention of his current employers. Every cloud has a silver lining, and that one enabled him to line his pockets not with silver, but with gold.

The gold had already been deposited in his numbered bank account in Zurich. Payment in advance was his personal insurance policy to prevent his associates from killing him to save the cost of his fee.

His pocket now held a small .32 pistol. Not that he contemplated treachery. But it was folly to go weaponless among armed men.

He went down into the ship's cavernous hold to inspect the arming of the explosives.

The air belowdecks was thick, oppressive, visible as a smoggy haze. Infrequent overhead spotlights cast long columns of light in the vast, dim space.

The explosives came in fifty-gallon canisters boxed four to a crate. The crates were stacked in big cubes, wrapped in chains and binders to prevent their shifting position even a slight degree. Stamped on the crates was the deceptive label, OLIVE OIL.

The armaments came from an old munitions cache left over from one of the frequent outbreaks of Greek-Turkish civil war on the island of Cyprus. The load was bought on the cheap, but it was no bargain.

After baking for a while in the humid hold, the plastique began to sweat. Dewlike beads of condensation, the concentrated liquid essence of C-4, sparkled on the canisters. Each highly volatile bead could generate a mini-blast capable of blowing off a man's hand. Just one could produce a chain reaction exploding the entire load.

The beads were mopped up—carefully. But they kept reappearing.

It seemed superfluous to have Hasim and Ali, the

demolitions men, rig detonators to key trigger points in the stacked crates, but unstable explosives are quirky. Nobody wanted to take the chance that the blast might fail to come off on schedule.

The Lebanese youths laughed and joked as they worked. Farmingdale frowned. "Those lads take it rather lightly, don't they?"

"To show fear is unmanly. They are not afraid," Mokhtar said.

"There's nothing unmanly about caution. Not with this load. It's a tinderbox. I don't mind telling you, I wouldn't have taken the job if I'd known the condition of the cargo. Not unless I was paid a damned sight more."

"My principal had been told of their inferior quality. Heads will roll . . . but that need not concern us."

"I still feel that I deserve a bonus for this extremely hazardous run—"

"Come now, Captain. You were handsomely paid, enough to cover any risk. Besides, my principal holds his contracts to be ironclad."

"By the way, old boy, just who is this mysterious principal of yours? I'm in this just as deep as you. It's only right that I should know who hired me."

"If you knew my principal's identity, old boy, you would soon be very dead," Mokhtar said. And he smiled.

Unnerving smile, that, thought Farmingdale. Was it a trick of the imagination, or were his teeth actually filed into points?

Farmingdale cleared his throat. "Yes. Right. Well, we'll speak no more about it, then. It doesn't matter to me who—good lord!"

Hasim needed a detonator. Ali tossed him one. Hasim caught it, then went back to work.

The detonators were tricky and volatile too. Had

Hasim fumbled the catch and dropped it, it all could have ended right there.

Farmingdale paled. "That bloody fool could have blown us all up!"

"Yes, that was quite careless." Mokhtar spoke sharply to the two Shiites. The captain's spotty Arabic wasn't enough to translate the actual words, but their meaning was quite clear. Silly grins melted off the faces of Ali and Hasim. Straight-faced, serious, all clowning put aside, they went back to work.

"I think I'll run along back to the bridge," the captain said, and did.

Chastened, Ali and Hasim finished their task with swift efficiency. Presently, they and Mokhtar emerged from the hold. After its gloomy menace, the bright sunlight was as exhilarating as a stay of execution.

"One moment, please," Mokhtar said.

Ali stared longingly at the getaway boat bobbing astern. "Time grows short, brother. Should we not be gone?"

"Your recklessness endangered our mission."

Hasim's high spirits staged a comeback. "Allah did not will that we die below. Is that not so? Else we would not be here, speaking of it."

"True." Mokhtar reached as if to loosen his collar. "Allah wills that you die here, by my hand."

Mokhtar drew the dagger sheathed in the back of his jacket, between his shoulder blades. Slashing down and across, he cut Hasim's throat with such force that the Lebanese was nearly decapitated.

Gurgling his disbelief, Hasim flopped to the deck.

"No!" Horrified, Ali backed off, spun, and ran.

A deft snap of the wrist shook the blood off the blade. Mokhtar's toss sent it whirling through the air. It thudded home in Ali's broad back.

Ali jerked, staggered forward a few more paces,

reaching for the knife. Before he took hold of it, death took hold of him.

As chance would have it, Captain Farmingdale rounded a corner and came on the scene just in time for Ali to fall facedown at his feet. "What—what the devil goes on here?"

Mokhtar wrenched his blade free from the corpse, wiping it clean on Ali's shirt before sheathing it. "Hasim and Ali chose to stay on board."

"Hmmm? Oh, right. Can't say I blame you, old boy. Those laddies took it too lightly for my liking."

Mokhtar and the captain went up to wheelhouse, moving quickly. With the explosives now armed, the sooner they quit the ship, the better.

Standing beside Gorgias at the wheel was Ensign Binayah Kerfud, formerly of the Libyan navy. The sad-eyed, gangly young man volunteered for the mission to strike a blow at the Zionist allies of the Great Satan, the United States.

"Any bother?" Farmingdale asked.

"No," Gorgias replied.

"Our cover story is working like a bloody charm. The Israelis still believe that we're en route to Jaffa with a load of olive oil! Damned clever chap, your boss—clever, and thorough, too!"

"I know it," Mokhtar said. "Soon, the world will know it."

The *Melina*'s final destination was the golden strip of beach belonging to Tel Aviv's luxury hotels, a beach now crowded with hundreds if not thousands of tourists and locals. Kerfud would pilot the shallow-draft ship into the shallows, running it aground.

What would happen next was a matter of conjecture in some particulars, though the grisly outcome was never in doubt. The cargo might explode from the impact of hitting the bottom, or it might not.

If it exploded, well and good. If not, Kerfud would activate his hand-held radio transmitter, keying a frequency that would trigger first the detonators, then the tons of explosives.

The *Melina* was the world's biggest seagoing antipersonnel bomb. The blast would fragment her into a storm of white-hot steel whose every scrap and shard would be a lethal missile. Spectators crowding the shore would be mowed down like weeds under a scythe.

"You are ready?" Mokhtar asked.

"I am ready," Kerfud said.

Mokhtar embraced him. "We shall meet again in Paradise."

"I will not fail!"

Captain Farmingdale threw the Libyan a snappy salute. "Carry on!"

Gorgias shook Kerfud's hand, muttering, "Good luck—er, that is, uh, I mean . . . well, you know what I mean."

"Come on, let's get the bloody hell out of here!" Farmingdale said.

Captain, first mate, and Mokhtar exited the wheelhouse. Mokhtar allowed himself one last glance. All was as it should be. Kerfud had assumed a heroic stance, aware of his central role and determined to make a good show. His gaze searched beyond this horizon, to the world to come.

Mokhtar was a great believer in backup systems. The captain had assured him it would be a simple matter to set the controls on automatic to steer the ship to shore, but Mokhtar mistrusted machinery. He was happier with Kerfud piloting the final run.

He mistrusted people no less than machinery. That was why he carried a second transmitter, a twin of the one in Kerfud's possession. If the Libyan's nerve failed, if he deviated from his suicide run, Mokhtar would detonate the bomb by remote control.

And Kerfud knew it. Doomed in any case, he had every incentive to die a glorious hero and martyr.

Mokhtar left him there, standing at the wheel.

No sense in dawdling now. Mokhtar exhibited some haste in going along the starboard gallery. To himself he said, "Thus begins Operation Ifrit!"

Gorgias and the captain stood at the rail, Farmingdale scanning the southern horizon through a pair of binoculars.

Odd . . . actually, the operation should already have begun with the spectacular destruction of the Shamash complex. But Mokhtar heard no distant echo of explosions. Hand shading his eyes from the glare, he searched south. No smoky inferno delighted his eyes.

What he did see was the Superbo speeding back toward him.

"I say! That's damned peculiar!" Farmingdale's puzzlement gave way to outrage as the binoculars were torn from his grasp. "Here, now, there's no cause for rudeness!"

Mokhtar stared through the eyepieces.

The powerboat was speeding along, skimming over the waves, carving a white wake across the waters as it followed an irresistible trajectory straight toward the ship.

Nick Carter had company on his showdown run. Elias was along for the ride.

Certifiably dead, the Basque was bound upright in the seat beside Carter, strapped in position by a pair of web belts, a rifle wedged in his arms.

It was simple, desperate strategy—a decoy to draw enemy fire. The shipboard defenders didn't know Elias wasn't in on it with Carter, didn't even know he was dead. He looked alive enough, from a distance. The decoy corpse doubled the targets while halving Carter's chances of catching a bullet.

The rocket launchers were the most sophisticated available. Carter had one primed, its covers off, sighting and trigger mechanisms in place. But the weapon required the use of both hands for proper operation.

Carter solved that problem. He hunched down low, offering the least possible target. He was wedged in his seat, legs folded, bare feet pressing the wheel. The armed launcher's rest was fitted snugly to his shoulder, its flared muzzle clearing the boat's venturi windshield. He opened up the Superbo and came on full speed ahead.

The sweep of the northern horizon receded; the ship loomed before him. He could make out figures darting along the ways, frantically gesturing figures.

They knew he was coming for them.

The *Melina* grew and grew, its black hull curving up. It blotted out more and more seascape, filling his field of vision.

They were shooting at him. Bullets whipped overhead, buzzing like angry bumblebees. A whole hive of them. One shattered the windshield. Carter's sunglasses shielded his eyes from the debris.

The bow shuddered from the impact of a line of slugs tearing into it. Elias jerked this way and that as bullets ripped him, shredding head and shoulders.

Still the Superbo came on. Carter was too close to miss his target. If he came much closer, it would be impossible for him to pull out in time.

Captain Farmingdale wrung his hands, groaning, "What a bloody cock-up!"

Mokhtar's men lined the rail, working their assault rifles like fire hoses, pumping out streams of slugs. Their aim was no good, the vast majority of shots whizzing harmlessly over the target or raking the water around it.

"He's going to ram us!" Farmingdale cried.

Gorgias turned on the captain. "You damned Jonah!"

"Are you mad? What are you doing?! No, don't—"

Snarling, the first mate tried to strangle the skipper.

Mokhtar screamed for somebody to give him a rifle, but his men were too excited to pay him any heed. Finally, he tore one out of the hands of a startled shooter.

Born and bred a desert raider—and what a long way he had come from that desert in the service of his master—Mokhtar had owned a rifle from his earliest youth. The weapon was his instrument; he could play it like a virtuoso. He was a crack marksman who could hit anything he could see.

His palms slapped stock and barrel as he snatched up the rifle from his man. With the fluidity of effortless skill, he drew a bead on Carter's head.

And that was the last thing Mokhtar ever did, because the Killmaster fired first.

WHOOSH!

The launcher lurched with the backblast, a finned rocket streaking from the muzzle.

Carter didn't wait for the results. Dropping the launcher, he grabbed the wheel with both hands, spinning it hard to starboard, powering into a near 90-degree turn.

The rocket hit the *Melina* squarely amidships, about eight feet above the waterline. It hit like Thor's hammer.

Steel bulkheads imploded under the impact of the armor-piercing shell, which exploded inside the ship. That blast, mighty as it was, was only the spark that touched off the powder keg.

Split seconds later, an infinitely greater blast was unleashed as the *Melina*'s explosive cargo ignited.

Canister after canister of C-4 instantly volatilized into heat, gas, and pressure waves. The series of explosions came so quickly that it seemed one ever-increasing roar.

No ship could contain that incandescent fury. Cataracts of flame poured out of hatchways and ventilator shafts. The deck and upper works were pulverized in the searing fireball. Fields of flame segmented the hull, slicing it apart at the seams. The remains of the *Melina* formed a small black shape at the base of an enormous pillar of fire.

The tremendous expanding pressure wave flung the Superbo high in the air. Before Carter could think to jump clear, he *was* clear, flying one way while the boat went in a different direction.

A giant invisible hand slam-dunked Carter into the sea, stuffing him down, down, down.

The water changed color as he dropped into the depths, going from yellow-green, to dark green, to greenish black. Currents sported with him, buffeting, flinging him this way and that.

The water vibrated with muted booming as the explosions kept coming.

Carter was dazed, confused. Which way was up?

Silver bubbles streamed past him, rising. They issued from his nose and mouth. He breathed water. He was drowning!

He followed the bubbles, using powerful kicks and strokes. The chill uniform blackness surrounding him seemed to have no end. After a timeless interval it lightened, going through the color gradient in reverse, from black to green to yellow-green.

His head finally broke the surface. He coughed, choking. Brackish water spewed from mouth and nostrils, painful, burning.

Day had become night. A pall of black smoke blotted the sky, dimmed the sun. Red firelight underlit the clouds, bloodied the waters. Debris rained down from above.

What remained of the *Melina*'s hull split in two. Fireworks spurted from the fast-sinking twin hulks. Oil leaked from the wreck like black blood, spreading over the troubled waters.

As the halves went down, a whirlpool formed. Suction tugged at Carter, gently at first, then greedily, demanding.

He struck out, swimming away from the widening vortex, taking care not to swallow any oil.

Isolated patches of oil burned, quickly linking up in a fiery blanket. Heat tingled on Carter's flesh. The water grew warmer, much warmer.

The flaming ring was hard on his heels, just short of overtaking him. He swam submerged.

When he came up to breathe, flames and choking smoke surrounded him. He sucked a gasping breath, went under, and swam until he thought his lungs would burst. Better that, he thought, than to have them seared by oil fire.

When he finally surfaced, he was beyond the flames and the swirling vortex. Treading water, he watched the *Melina*'s remains sink out of sight. Hissing steam clouds rose to join the smoke.

Anxiety struck him. He grabbed his right arm, relieved to find Hugo's comforting steel securely nestled in place. The blade was an old friend and he would have hated to lose it.

It was funny how things worked out, Carter mused. The *Melina* met her fate not far from the bustling port of Jaffa. Jaffa—the ancient city was known as Joppa in biblical times—was where the original Jonah had set sail on the ill-fated voyage that landed him in the belly of the whale.

Captain Farmingdale might have appreciated the irony. Then again, he might not.

Carter did.

The shore seemed a long way off. Carter swam toward it. He hadn't gone very far when an Israeli patrol boat fished him out of the sea.

FIVE

On the night before the *Melina* incident, Avram Maltz, deputy assistant to the Minister of Maritime Trade, tried to take it on the lam.

Maltz skulked in the shadows of the underground parking garage beneath a Tel Aviv luxury high-rise apartment complex. Fourteen floors above, his wife of twenty-one years slept and snored, oblivious of the fact that her husband was flying the coop.

And good riddance! Maltz thought. Abandoning bovine Esther was the only good to come out of this unholy mess.

He traveled light. Aside from the clothes on his back, he carried only his passport, papers, and an attaché case crammed with cash.

He was getting out while he still could. He must have been insane to get in as deep as he had. Disgrace, utter ruin would have been better. His "associates" dealt out murder as casually as a traffic cop hands out citations.

Even Lemniak was afraid. Lemniak, with his international connections and his quartet of big, tough, well-armed bodyguards. That was the clincher for Maltz. If a big shot like Lemniak was trying to wriggle out and cut a private deal to save his own neck—and he was—then what chance did he, Maltz, have?

Less than none, but he didn't know that yet.

The deserted parking garage was unsettling, eerie at the midnight hour. Its elderly attendant was cozily installed in a subbasement room, sleeping on the job, as usual. Maltz had passed him earlier when he'd tiptoed down to the garage.

Maltz waited on the bottom landing of the stairs, peeking through the slightly ajar fire door. Looking down the ranks of parked cars, he saw no one. That was comforting, since he was sure he'd been followed for the last few days.

He wanted to be absolutely positive he was alone, but he couldn't wait forever. He had a plane to catch, a flight to New York City. When he arrived safely at his destination, he'd contact the authorities and tip them off.

Maltz made his break. He darted out the door, hustling down the aisles to his car.

Banks of overhead fluorescent lights hummed, flickered. From somewhere came the distant sound of machinery. At the garage's far end lay its exit, a broad archway opening onto a ramp rising to street level. Through it poured the nighttime sounds of the restless city.

His car was parked in the middle of the garage. Maltz was fumbling with his keys when a whistle shrilled.

He started guiltily, looking up. The whistle came from the street, but he saw no one.

Something flew into the garage.

Maltz froze, then thawed. The wind must have blown a child's kite down from the street. Only—there was no wind. No kite, either.

It was a bird, its wings flapping, a huge bird the likes of which he'd never seen. Flying straight for him, with a four-foot wingspan, gold and brown and tan speckled body, wickedly curved beak and outstretched talons.

A bird of prey. Swift, unerring, with deadly intent.

"Shoo! Shoo!" Maltz didn't want to betray his presence by shouting, but he was afraid. Terrified. Especially since the big bird closed in on a collision course.

He threw up his arms, shielding his face with the attaché case, then screamed as razor-sharp talons ripped his hands.

The bird hovered, flew away, dipped a wing to wheel around a concrete support post, then came back for another pass.

Maltz flailed at it, the hovering bird easily avoiding his clumsy swings. The attaché case cracked against a car's fender and popped open, spilling stacks of bills all over the floor.

The bird went for his head, ripping, tearing. Each talon was like a four-inch barbed fishhook rending his flesh. Half-blinded by blood, fear, and pain, Maltz covered his face with his hands.

The peregrine's talons tore open Maltz's soft throat.

Holding his neck, trying to stem the gush of blood, sobbing, gurgling, Maltz stumbled down the aisle, kicking wads of currency, careening off cars, dying.

Each beat of his furiously pounding heart sent fresh gouts of blood pulsing from his savaged throat, his rended veins and arteries. He gagged, spat, toppled, sprawled, convulsed.

A high-pitched whistle again sounded. Responding to its master's call, the peregrine ended its attack, wheeled. A few flaps of its powerful wings and it glided through the arched exit, into the street, and out of sight.

Avram Maltz bled to death before help arrived.

Israeli homicide detectives and forensic specialists, wise in the ways of violent death, were forced to confront a new and novel technique, unique in their experience:

Murder by falcon.

• • •

At noon of the following day, David Hawk occupied a table at an outdoor eatery in the pleasant seaside resort town of Lulav. The Etrog Café was famed throughout the land for its house specialty, the succulent lemon chicken. Hawk lunched on blander fare, fillet of sole and a salad. He wanted to concentrate on the forthcoming meeting, not a meal.

Situated north of Tel Aviv and south of Herzeliyya, Lulav was charming, chic, and not a little expensive. The café was set back from the corner of an intersection in the town's elegant shopping district. Ranged on both sides of the thoroughfare, boutiques and shops vended their wares: silverwork, leather goods, ceramics, jewelry, antiquities, a host of handicrafts made by talented artisans. Street traffic was light, pedestrians were many.

The café's main room was of white stucco, trimmed with dark wood beams and pierced with round windows. Its patio held twenty tables, most of them occupied. Each table came equipped with a parasol that could be hand-cranked open or closed; Hawk's was open. Its shade and an occasional sea breeze eased the heat of the day.

An attentive waiter removed Hawk's plate and brought him a fresh iced tea. The white-haired, keen-eyed American idly rolled a cigar in his fingers as he scanned his fellow diners.

All in all, they were a typical sampling of tourists and natives, reassuring in their sun-splashed normality.

Not far from where he sat, a young woman soldier sipped a soft drink and leafed through a book of poetry. Her insignia marked the fatigue-clad beauty as a corporal in the reserves. *She must be on a break or off duty,* thought Hawk. Her Galil auto-rifle stood near at hand, propped against the pavilion's waist-high balustrade.

In Israel, one quickly grew used to the sight of male

and female soldiers stationed at even the most peaceful-
looking places. Security was paramount.

Her image touched memories in Hawk, reminding
him of some of the women he'd known, beautiful and
dangerous and brave. During World War II, when he
was one of Wild Bill Donovan's OSS crew, parachuting
behind enemy lines to link up with resistance partisans,
he'd known a lady of the maquis, Marie . . . she'd gone
to the wall of a Gestapo firing squad in January 1944.

Hawk sighed. The corporal must have heard him. She
casually glanced up. He smiled. She smiled, too, then
went back to her book.

What became of that raw recruit of so long ago, the
reckless young David Hawk who thought that raw nerve
and a fast gun were enough to save the world?

He was now the chief of AXE, still sticking his neck
out some forty-odd years later.

Hawk was the only one at his table, but he was not
alone. Two of his top agents were here with him. One of
them approached his table.

Andy Stanton was a husky, handsome young fellow,
an ex-Navy SEAL recruited by AXE who had distin-
guished himself in the field. He was pressing hard to at-
tain the coveted Killmaster ranking.

He looked like a typical American tourist enjoying a
jaunt to the Holy Land. Threading the aisles between
tables, he sidestepped to avoid a platter-laden waiter, a
purposeful detour taking him right past Hawk.

Andy whispered in an aside, "Griff spotted our
man." He kept on walking, not breaking stride. He
eyed the corporal with open admiration. Her slow,
sidelong glance showed she did not object to the attention from the big, good-looking man.

At the other side of the raised patio, a wide gap
opened in the balustrade, allowing broad, shallow stairs
to spill to the sidewalk.

Up those stairs scurried a disreputable-looking character clad in a wrinkled white suit and straw Borsalino hat. Head hunched forward, body stooped, hands jammed in pockets, he crossed the pavilion as if eager to get out of the sun as soon as possible.

It took Hawk an instant to place this rumpled, nervous man as the once suave, elegant Delos Lemniak.

Looking neither left, right, nor up, he weaved past tables and patrons, on the verge of collision a half-dozen times yet somehow always veering clear at the last possible second.

At least one thing about Lemniak hadn't changed. He was still skating by on the skin of his teeth.

Lemniak made a beeline for Hawk's table. He panted, out of breath, "Holloway, good to see you."

"Delos," Hawk acknowledged.

Delos Lemniak had been bouncing around the Levant and the eastern Mediterranean for decades. He was a fixer and a bagman, dealmaker, profiteer, corruptor. A clearinghouse for information. Everyone's friend, and no one's friend. His integrity was well known: he was scrupulously faithful to the highest bidder, regardless of race, creed, or cause.

He knew Hawk as "Bart Holloway." Holloway was a cover identity established by Hawk well over a generation ago, back before the founding of AXE. As Holloway, Hawk had made many useful connections, and he found it advantageous to resurrect the legend from time to time.

Such as now. Lemniak "knew" Holloway was CIA. Working through a cutout—a third party—Lemniak sent a message requesting a meeting. This was it.

Had Hawk suspected for one second that Lemniak knew his true identity as the head of AXE, the rendezvous would not have taken place. As himself, David Hawk was number one on a dozen kill lists.

Despite the precautions, Hawk was taking a risk. But he relished this game of multiple identities and the chance to work in the field once more.

Besides, Lemniak just might have something of value.

They shook hands. Lemniak's was soft, moist, warm. It felt like a boiled fish, and was so sweaty that Hawk's hand came away wet. Hawk wiped it clean on a napkin while Lemniak sat down. He sat facing the street.

The waiter swooped down on them. Lemniak ordered a Campari and soda. No sooner was it delivered than he gulped it down, then immediately ordered another round.

"Well, Delos, what's on your mind?" Hawk said.

"I have something to sell. Something big."

"With a price to match, no doubt."

"It's worth it."

"I'm listening."

Lemniak mopped his face with a limp handkerchief. It was already soaked, so rubbing his face with it only served to move the sweat around.

"My price is one million in gold, plus a new identity in the country of my choice," he said.

Hawk's smile was ice-cold. "Why not ask for the moon, too, while you're at it?"

"I don't understand."

"Back in the States, our government is running up a trillion-dollar deficit. Uncle Sammy is way in debt and it's time for belt-tightening. Not that I could have gotten you a million even in the salad days."

"A million is cheap for what I've got," Lemniak hissed.

"What have you got? You know how the game is played, Delos. We don't buy a pig in a poke. Give me some idea of what you've got, then we'll talk."

"All right. I—"

Lemniak gave a violent start as two gaily shrieking youngsters dashed past the table. Seated a few tables away, their mother gave Hawk one of those what-can-you-do? looks.

Lemniak stopped shaking and got a grip on himself. He was in sad shape, a bundle of nerves.

"Militant Islam," he said.

Hawk sighed. "If that's your big secret, we might as well call it a day. We've known about Militant Islam since the organization was formed in Qom six months ago. Nice seeing you again, Delos. The drinks are on me."

Lemniak was under pressure and Hawk tightened the screws by making as if he were about to leave.

"Don't be so cocksure, Holloway." Lemniak was rattled, and showing it. "What about Operation Ifrit? Does that mean anything to you?"

Indeed it did. Ever since the Big Three of the radical Islamic states—Libya, Iran, and Syria—founded the Militant Islam group in the holy city of Qom, the Middle East had been abuzz with rumors of a new wave of terrorist assaults. The action was code-named Operation Ifrit.

Not coincidentally, the last communication AXE received from Agent N3 stated that he was following up a hot lead concerning that same operation. That was over six weeks ago. Since then, Carter hadn't been seen or heard from. The earth seemed to have swallowed him up.

Something of Hawk's poker face slipped. He showed a flicker of interest, and Lemniak picked up on it, which was encouraging, demonstrating as it did that the old con artist was not too far gone to have lost all critical judgment. That was why Hawk engineered the deliberate slip in the first place. Perhaps Lemniak's judgment could be relied on in other matters as well.

Lemniak pounced. "I see that does mean something to you! You wouldn't be in Israel right now if not for Ifrit."

"Why don't you sell whatever you've got to the Israelis?"

"Don't be absurd! They don't toss that kind of money around."

"Neither do we."

"Besides, I don't trust them. They're compromised."

"Compromised?"

"Penetrated. Infiltrated. Subverted."

Hawk did not bother to hide his disbelief. "By whom?"

"Ah-hah." Lemniak waved a chiding finger. "That's part of what I've got to sell."

"That might be worth something—if it's true."

"It's true, all right, and it's only part of the package I'm offering. Israel's not the only target, you know. America's Arab allies are slated for punishment too."

"Tell me something I don't know."

"What's a paltry million dollars compared to the toll in lives and property you'll save? Would you have paid a million to block Khomeini's rise to power? To save Sadat? To keep your Marines from being blown up in Beirut? Of course you would. I tell you, those debacles are child's play compared to Ifrit."

"That brings us back to the big question. What have you got?" Hawk asked.

"The boss of terror." Lemniak was smug, scenting victory in the negotiations. "The linchpin, the mastermind behind the entire plot."

"Who is it?"

"I know who he is and where he is. He's not far from here." A shudder ripped Lemniak's smugness. "There's still time for you to kill him if you act now. Don't try to take him alive. He's too dangerous for that. Kill him."

"Who?"

"I'll tell you that much. It won't do you any good without the rest of the information." Lemniak leaned forward. "His name is R—"

Gunfire interrupted the revelation.

• • •

Petra Kelly didn't like rush jobs. They were particularly dicey here in the Land of Zion, where universal military service and an armed citizen-soldiery stacked the deck against a successful action.

But she liked dying even less. Her master enforced a uniform policy regarding such infractions as disobedience, insubordination, failure to carry out an assignment. Offenders were executed. Messily.

She was the sole daughter and eldest child of a wealthy Dublin tradesman. Her revolt against affluence and privilege took her into the Provo wing of the IRA. She concealed her family background, fearful that she would not be taken as a serious comrade because of it. After she made her first kill, nobody ever told her to make tea again.

She did her murderous work well. Who would imagine that such a lovely green-eyed colleen was a terrorist? Northern Ireland proved too small a venue for one of her talents, so she got on the international circuit, wreaking havoc throughout Europe and the Mediterranean.

And then one day she got involved in Operation Ifrit, and since then, her life was no longer her own. She belonged body and soul to her master.

He never took her, never even touched her. He desired only that she continue doing what she was so good at: killing. And killing, and killing, and killing.

She liked the work, but she feared him. Quite an individual, this man who terrified the terrorists.

Petra was leggy and lissome. Her short red hair was netted and flattened under a blond wig. Oversize sunglasses masked much of her elfin face, giving her a vaguely buglike look.

She wore a sleeveless white V-necked dress that displayed the inner curves of her firm, pert breasts. Slung over her shoulder was a large woven straw bag, the sort available at every souvenir stand, a type used by many tourists.

Petra was not alone. Joining her on the job was Ulli Schwob, late of the German Red Army Faction. Ulli was ten years her senior, half a head taller, and some fifty pounds heavier. She was built like the Brünnhilde of a third-rate Wagnerian opera company.

Ulli also wore a light summer dress, and, like Petra, toted a straw bag. The pair sat at a table not far from Hawk.

Ulli kept craning her neck, peering down into the street. Her vigil was now rewarded.

A taxi pulled up to the curb, disgorging four armed men. They looked worried but grimly intent on carrying out their business.

The master had provided plenty of firepower for this job.

Petra and Ulli went to work. They stood up and started shooting.

While he was verbally fencing with Lemniak, Hawk's eyes had been in constant motion, systematically scanning his surroundings for the jarring detail that spells danger. Something about Petra and Ulli had nagged at his sixth sense, and his gaze kept returning to them.

Perhaps it was the matching straw totes sported by the two innocent-seeming women. There was no reason why companions might not have identical bags, but surely it was more than coincidence that they both had reached inside them at the same time—

Gunfire crackled on the street and sidewalk.

Ulli and Petra fished Uzis out of their bags and stood up. The unexpected gunplay behind them threw off their timing.

Hawk was already in motion.

He didn't waste time on shouted warnings. Even as he

threw himself out of his chair, he pulled Lemniak down and to the side.

The deadly pair's opening rounds passed overhead, missing the two prone men but striking a waiter. The café's outdoor patio was transformed into a scene of instant chaos. Pandemonium.

Tables were overturned, panicked patrons threw themselves flat on the floor, shrieks and sobs counterpointed the *rat-a-tat-tat* of high-velocity submachine gun rounds.

Yoga workouts kept Hawk supple, but the drop to the floor jarred his bones. He tipped over the table, its heavy rim cracking the stones with a deafening crash.

Lemniak was whimpering and babbling at the same time.

Adjusting her line of fire, Petra held her Uzi low, sweeping the slugs toward Lemniak. Bullets gouged a trail of holes across the stone floor.

Something totally unexpected happened to Petra. She was shot. Twice. She went down.

Now where the hell did that come from? Hawk wondered. From the corner of his eye he saw Andy Stanton crouching low, snapping off shots.

Good boy. He'd make Killmaster yet, if they all lived through this engagement.

Ulli took out the corporal early on, or so she thought. The beautiful sabra's right arm was half shot off at the shoulder, but somehow she got her Galil into play.

She poured a burst into Ulli. Ulli put up her hands as if they could prevent the slugs from hitting her. She went down in a hail of bullets.

The quartet of backup gunmen had run into trouble as soon as they piled out of the taxi. Trouble's name was Griff. The whole shooting match went off ahead of schedule because the black AXE agent started blasting when the killers stepped out on the sidewalk.

Only two members of the original foursome survived

the gunplay with Griff. The other two sprawled dead on the pavement.

Griff ducked behind a tree, trading shots with the taxi driver, who used his cab for cover.

There was a lull, an almost silent pause.

Lemniak stood up.

"Don't!" Hawk grabbed for Lemniak's leg from his prone position but missed. Lemniak scuttled toward the main building.

The corporal slumped out of her seat, dead, her weapon skittering on the flagstones. Hawk crawled to it.

Lemniak didn't have far to go, only a few more paces, but it was too far.

The last two gunmen stormed the pavilion. They came on shooting.

Lemniak had almost reached safety when both gunmen opened up on him at the same time. He went down.

And so did they. Andy Stanton hit one twice. Hawk brought the corporal's Galil back into play, firing from the prone position. It still held half a clip, which he emptied into the killers.

Griff ran out of ammo and had to reload. The taxi driver jumped in his cab and threw it in gear.

Petra Kelly was down, but not out. One of Stanton's bullets had blown a chunk out of her upper arm. The other hit not her, but her weapon, tearing it from her hand so hard that her finger was broken by the trigger guard. Shock had set in; she hardly felt her injuries. She had the sense to play possum until there was a lull in the shooting.

She jumped up, a blur of motion as she vaulted the pavilion wall.

Stanton shot at her—or rather he pulled the trigger at her, the hammer falling on an empty chamber. In the confusion he had forgotten to keep track of his shots, and now he didn't have any more.

Petra ran screaming to the cab. "Wait! Wait! Don't leave me!"

She had not time to open the door. She just threw herself headfirst through an open window while the cab was moving. Her long legs jutted out of the right rear window as the cab took off in a screaming start.

Tires screeched, smoking, burning rubber. The cab took the corner on two wheels, zooming into the distance.

Stanton hurried over to Hawk. "You okay, sir?"

"Yes."

He helped Hawk to his feet. "You're bleeding."

"Just cuts. I'm all right. Are they all dead?"

"Jeez, I don't know. Wait—there's Griff!"

Griff was a cautious man. Gun in hand, he warily circled the two Hawk had taken down. They were dead. Ulli, too.

"Looks like it's all over but the postmortems," Griff said.

The innocent bystanders shakily picked themselves up, not quite believing they had come through it alive.

A woman shrieked, raw and piercing. The mother Hawk had seen earlier. One of her children had been hit.

"Holy hell," Stanton whispered. "What a mess!"

Lemniak was still alive. He'd been mortally wounded, but he was holding on as long as he could.

Hawk, kneeling beside him, gently asked, "Who?"

Lemniak's hands shot up, grabbed Hawk's shirt front, pulled his head down. His mouth worked, laboring to form a word, the name.

Hawk tried again. "Who?"

"Reguiba," Lemniak wheezed. Then he died.

SIX

Israeli intelligence has a twin-chambered heart. Mossad handles foreign operations. Internal security is the province of *Sherut Habitachon*, known as the Shin Bet, or SB.

SB personnel refer to their outfit as "the Institute." Heading the Institute's Counterforce Antiterrorism unit was Dr. Chaim Bar-Zohar. Bar-Zohar looked like an intellectual jazz musician.

"You're a very naughty fellow, Hawk," he said.

It was the middle of the afternoon following the Café Etrog bloodbath. Bar-Zohar brought Hawk not to Institute headquarters, but to one of his unit's safe houses, an underground module located below an antiquarian bookseller's shop. The not overly large shelter maintained a permanent party of five, not including visitors and special guests.

Bar-Zohar went on, "Here we are, working together on a joint action, and then you elude my men to strike off on your own. Not very neighborly, I'd say."

"It wasn't very neighborly of you to have me followed in the first place," Hawk said.

"You didn't have much trouble shaking the tail.

Besides, you know that when they're not spying on their enemies, friends spy on friends.''

"How true."

"It's not that I object to your unauthorized sortie in my bailiwick. But imagine the consequences if you had been wounded or worse, God forbid. How would I have explained that to the Prime Minister? To your President?"

"He'd understand," Hawk said. "He likes initiative."

"So we've noticed," Bar-Zohar said dryly. "Well, you came out of it all right. It's too bad about Lemniak, though. We very much wanted to question him about his friend Avram Maltz."

"Who's he?" Hawk asked.

"Every organization has a key man, the fellow who really gets all the work done. In the Ministry of Maritime Trade, Maltz was that man. Unfortunately, he was working for someone besides the department.

"He abused his influence to fake a manifest for the *Melina*, allowing it to come right up to the coast. It looks like Maltz was the inside man for the ring which has been smuggling vast quantities of weapons and explosives into the country."

"From your use of the past tense, I assume Maltz is history," Hawk said.

"You're right. The most bizarre thing about his life was the way he left it." Bar-Zohar paused, savoring the suspense. "He was killed by a raptor."

"A what?"

"A raptor," Bar-Zohar repeated. "A bird of prey, such as an eagle, a falcon, or—a hawk. I'm surprised you didn't know that, considering your name."

"I was merely expressing astonishment at such a grotesque cause of death."

"It is grotesque, isn't it," Bar-Zohar said with a slight shudder. "Most unusual. Our specialists are still narrowing it down, but they're inclined to believe it was a peregrine falcon. A falcon trained to kill humans. Now, what do you make of that?"

"It might tie in with something Lemniak told me," Hawk said.

"Yes? Do go on."

"I'll tell you later."

"All right, be mysterious. Pity Lemniak didn't come to us. We could have protected him."

"I'm not so sure," Hawk said. "That fits in with something else Lemniak told me."

"Sounds like you two had quite a little chat."

"We did, until it was interrupted. I'll give you all the particulars—"

"Later. I'm sure you have your reasons for being so cryptic. As it happens, I have a surprise of my own for you. Come right this way, please," Bar-Zohar directed.

Hawk followed Bar-Zohar down a narrow hall to a door. Opening it, Bar-Zohar said, "This is our lost and found department. We have something that belongs to you."

Hawk looked quizzically at the Israeli.

"Go right in."

Bar-Zohar stepped aside, holding the door so Hawk could enter first. Hawk crossed the threshold, stopping dead in his tracks when he saw the room's occupant.

"Nick!"

Carter wore clean clothes and had a warm meal in his belly. He was refreshed and ready to take on the world. He stood up and said, "Good afternoon, sir."

"It is now. It's good to see you, Nick. Damned good." Hawk shook Carter's hand.

Hawk's shining eyes betrayed his pleasure at the unexpected reunion, but he remembered himself in time to recover his mask of steely sardonicism.

"Some folks had just about given you up for lost."

"But not you, sir."

"I knew better. I said you were probably off on some desert isle with a lovely lady, enjoying yourself at the outfit's expense."

"Actually, that's not too far off the mark, sir," Carter said. "I've been taking a sea cruise—but most definitely not for pleasure. And it turned out to be no fun at all for my shipmates. I'll tell you all about it."

Hawk held up a hand. "Save it for later, Nick." He addressed Bar-Zohar. "I want my aides to hear this too. Also, do you have a secure conference room?"

"My dear Hawk, I like to think that all our rooms are secure," Bar-Zohar said.

"You just might have to rethink that. We need a room that is certified free of all surveillance and recording devices. Where do you go when you want to make a statement that you're positive will be off the record?"

"That'll be Room Five."

"Room Five it is," Hawk said.

"I'll go make the arrangements," Bar-Zohar said, and walked out.

Room 5 was spare, stark, sterile, and small. The white-walled box held an oblong table, chairs, and the machinery of debugging monitors, which now certified that the room was free and clear of any sort of electro-magnetic surveillance.

"I just can't credit Lemniak's statement that we've been penetrated," Bar-Zohar said.

"Somebody got to Maltz," Hawk pointed out.

"Yes, but that's the Ministry of Maritime Trade, not the Shin Bet. I can't believe it. It sounds like part of a disinformation plot to sow dissension and distrust between allies and in our own Institute. Suppose he had told you that AXE was penetrated. Would you have believed that?"

"That slaughterhouse at the café did give Lemniak's story a certain credibility," Hawk said.

Bar-Zohar was unhappy. "In any case, this room is secure, and I'll take personal responsibility for my aides."

"I'll vouch for my personnel," Hawk said.

"Then we can begin."

Present at the meeting, besides the two chiefs, were Carter, Griff, Stanton, and two of Bar-Zohar's most trusted assistants, Berger and Tigdal.

Berger was slight, sallow, cadaverous. Lieutenant Avi Tigdal's military background was evident right to the knife-sharp creases in his pants. He was big, bluff, tough, efficient.

Griff and Stanton were less inhibited than their boss in showing their pleasure at Carter's return. Griff ribbed Carter, "You sure picked a fine time to quit goofing off and come back to work."

Carter only smiled.

A message was delivered to Bar-Zohar, who gave the group the gist of it. "The four men who came to kill Lemniak have been identified."

"Who were they?"

"His bodyguards."

Hawk snorted. "Looks like someone made them a better offer."

"See what happens when you underpay your key personnel?" Stanton said.

"I think we can dispense with the jokes, Stanton."

"Uh, right. Sorry, sir."

"Any sign of the blond woman who escaped with the driver?" Griff asked.

"None," Bar-Zohar replied. "The taxi was found not far from the café. They must have switched to a second car. We're hunting high and low for them, but there are no leads as yet."

He turned to Carter. "I believe you have some background for us on the *Melina* incident?"

"Yes."

Carter quickly sketched a broad outline of the twisted trail he'd been following for months.

Posing as Solano, he worked the Italian beat, where the once dormant Red Brigade had been reborn with a vengeance. Infiltrating that limbo where the criminal and political underworlds intersect, he'd come to the attention of the top bosses of Italian terror, who recruited him for a very special action taking place outside that country: Operation Ifrit.

In Moslem lore, an *ifrit* was a demonic being similar to the genies of the *Arabian Nights*. Operation Ifrit would unleash the demon of destruction on the United States by punishing her allies.

The action was sponsored and paid for by the radical Militant Islam group. But carrying out the multinational terrorist offensive was the handiwork of one man, a shadowy master criminal who drew on a far-flung pool of murderous talent.

"I haven't been able to pin down his identity yet—"

"I may be able to help you on that, Nick," Hawk cut in. "But go on."

"I do have someone almost as good, though," Carter continued. "The big wheel who personally recruited me in Italy—the talent scout, you might call him—happens to be 'vacationing' right now at his villa in Lulav. I have a date with a lady friend in his entourage."

"Who is he?"

"Gianni Girotti," Carter said.

"Girotti?" Tigdal said. "That playboy? I don't believe it! Why, his idea of a revolutionary act is to go to dinner without a necktie!"

"You don't have to believe it," Carter said. "I know it's true. That dilettantish pose of his has fooled a lot of people."

"What are we waiting for? Let's pick him up and sweat him!" Berger said.

"He's tougher than he looks. You'll never get anything out of him by force," Carter cautioned.

"Have you got a better way?"

"As a matter of fact, yes," Carter said. "A plan that will not only net us Girotti and his pals, but which could lead us right to the top man."

"Now I'll throw in my two cents," Hawk said. "Before he died, Lemniak gave me a name, the mysterious Mr. Big behind Operation Ifrit. It didn't ring a bell with me, but maybe one of you can do better."

"Try us," Bar-Zohar said.

"Reguiba."

The name was met with a round of puzzled shrugs and head shakings.

"Reguiba," Bar-Zohar mused. "Reguiba, Reguiba, Reguiba." He looked up. "Who the devil is Reguiba?"

"I'm hurt," Petra Kelly whimpered. "Oh God, I'm hurt!"

"Shut up!" the taxi driver snapped. He no longer drove the taxi. They had ditched it a few blocks from the café, at the prearranged site where the second, getaway car waited. Now he drove that car, while Petra bled all over the back seat. They were one short jump ahead of the fast-tightening dragnet.

Petra pressed a wadded red rag to her shoulder wound to stem the flow of blood. The rag was yellow before she put it to use. Enough shock had worn off for her to feel pain, pain the likes of which she'd never known.

What went wrong? This couldn't be happening to her. It was unthinkable. A simple execution had turned into a rout, a massacre. She was outraged. The victims weren't supposed to shoot back; that wasn't how the game was played.

"God! I'm going to bleed to death!"

"Shut up!" the driver shouted again. It was difficult enough to thread the dockside streets and alleys of old

Jaffa without that Irish bitch shrieking her fool head off. Too bad it hadn't been blown off.

The driver was Dieter Ten Eyck, a Boer mercenary who'd signed on for Operation Ifrit, looking for big money and fast action. The money wasn't bad—though not nearly enough for what he'd just undergone—and the action was too fast. He could have been knocked over with a feather when that black guy had come out of nowhere to gun down two of Lemniak's treacherous bodyguards. After that, everything had gone to hell.

Ten Eyck couldn't take much more of Petra's wailing. If she didn't shut up, he'd—

But he didn't have to. They had arrived at the hideout, an abandoned warehouse on the waterfront.

Except it wasn't abandoned. Ten Eyck hit the horn with the heel of his hand, knocking out a snappy pattern of short and long honks that comprised the recognition code. The honking salute had a bright jauntiness that he found singularly inappropriate, considering the circumstances.

Moaning, Petra sat up. "Hurry! I'm bleeding to death!"

"Good."

"You lousy shit!"

Before she could get rolling on her tirade of abuse, a segmented steel door rolled ponderously upward, opening on the warehouse's dim interior.

Ten Eyck drove inside the sprawling, barnlike structure. The door rolled down behind him, slamming shut, locking the interior into semidarkness fitfully broken by small square windows set high, just under the eaves.

Ten Eyck and Petra were temporarily blinded by the sudden transition from light to dark. Others within were not so incapacitated.

Swift footsteps rushed the car from all sides. Figures surrounded the car.

Ten Eyck slid out of the front seat. "Am I glad to see

you fellows! We ran into a—*ugh!*"

He was pistol-whipped across the face, a stunning blow that felt like it broke his jaw. A second blow struck the side of his head with a crunching sound. He dropped.

His assailant didn't stop there, but stood over Ten Eyck, kicking him in the belly. Other hands tore open the back door and grabbed Petra.

"What are you doing?" she screeched. "Are you insane? We're on your side!"

"Slut!"

She screamed, and screamed again as she was hauled out of the car. Her wounded arm was wrenched so hard it felt dislocated. She nearly fainted, and wished she had. She was thrown down to the hard floor.

Somebody laughed.

Somebody else chuckled, a sound rich in sadistic relish.

The man kicking Ten Eyck in the belly jumped back to avoid the South African's spewing stream of vomit. "You pig!"

From overhead came the beat of heavy, fluttering wings. There was a pause in the violence. Petra stared at her circle of tormentors. She knew them better than she cared to, these members of the master's entourage.

Mansour was an Arab with a thin, mean face and a wiry, supple body. He was turned out like a fashion plate in a lightweight, beautifully tailored suit. Thin black leather gloves covered his hands, one of which gripped the pistol he'd used to club down Ten Eyck.

It was no mystery how the Camel had won his name. His resemblance to that beast was extraordinary. Elongated, gawky, he wore a red fez with a black tassel, and clutched a silenced pistol.

Idir was short, squat, solid, phlegmatic. Knife work was his specialty and his delight. He held one now, a wickedly curved and gleaming dagger, idly toying with it. He looked coy, almost flirtatious.

Lotah was Senegalese, a strapping coal-black giant whom a childhood ailment had left utterly hairless. Prior to joining the master, he'd worked as the royal executioner for various Mauritanian sheiks. He could lop off any head with a one-handed stroke from his scimitar. His hands were empty now; in and of themselves, they were lethal weapons.

Petra sobbed. "I don't understand! Why are you doing this?"

Ten Eyck, semiconscious, writhed and retched.

Into view came the man whom Idir, Mansour, the Camel, and Lotah acknowledged as their supreme master:

Reguiba.

Tall and thin, with the aquiline features and weathered skin of the desert-born, Reguiba was dressed all in black, deliberate in his movements, ominous. Sinister.

He wore a high-collared military-style tunic, trimmed at the collar and cuffs with gold braid. Baggy black cotton trousers were tucked into knee-high soft leather boots. Holstered on both hips were twin Colt .45s.

When he went abroad, on the street, he wore more conventional attire, of course. But here, in his domain of darkness, he dressed—and did—as he pleased.

"Say the word, O perfect master, and these dogs are dead," Mansour said.

"Were they followed?" Reguiba asked.

"We weren't followed!" Petra cried. "I swear, we weren't followed!"

She cowered as Mansour moved to kick her. Reguiba halted him with a slight nod. His men were most attentive to his every wish.

Again, he asked if the pair were followed. Lotah shook his head. That satisfied Reguiba.

Ten Eyck was in no condition to talk. Reguiba went to Petra. "Do not rise. I prefer to look down at you.

Your handling of the Lemniak kill was, let us say, less than competent.''

"But we got him!" Petra protested.

"But he almost escaped. I sent six to kill one. Two came back.''

"The target was supposed to be soft! We didn't know he was protected!''

"I will tell you something else you did not know. The man Lemniak met at the café is an American spy.''

That information made Petra feel even sicker. "How —how do you know that?''

"It does not matter how I know it, so long as I know it,'' Reguiba said.

"The night has a thousand eyes. Reguiba has ten thousand eyes!'' Mansour announced. He was a great flatterer.

"Had you the wit to slay the spy along wtih Lemniak, I might have let you live,'' Reguiba said. "But as it is . . .''

He did not complete the sentence, nor did he need to. Not all his men spoke English, but all knew when their master had decreed death. They were all smiles, like whorehouse patrons waiting in the parlor for their turn to come up.

"Why me?'' Petra sobbed. "It's not my fault! What about the others?''

"They have paid the price of failure. So will you.'' Reguiba indicated Ten Eyck, jackknifed on the floor. "So will he.''

Reguiba's men disputed the method of dispatch. Mansour said, "Why not shoot them?''

"Why waste bullets on the likes of them?'' Lotah wanted to know. "These hands will snap their pale, thin necks.''

"Our way was ever the way of the knife!'' Idir maintained. "Cut their throats and be done with it.''

"Too simple,'' the Camel said. "Too easy.''

Reguiba tended to agree with the Camel. Between the botched Lemniak kill, and the *Melina*'s harmless destruction at sea, he was in an ill humor and required some amusing diversion.

Handling a length of rope, Reguiba remarked, "How thin is the cord which binds us to life!"

He knotted a pair of nooses at the ends of the rope. The rope was tossed over a rafter beam, the nooses dangling level with one another. Benches were set under each noose.

Petra and Ten Eyck were set on the benches, facing each other, their hands tied behind their backs. The nooses were fixed around their necks with loving care.

Idir tied a heavy cement block to Petra's ankles, resting it on the bench. It would offset Ten Eyck's heavier weight. The victims had to be evenly balanced for the game to succeed.

The Camel pointed out that Petra was wounded, while Ten Eyck had two good arms.

"That is true." Reguiba drew his pistol and shot Ten Eyck in the arm. The booming report knocked dust down from the rafters.

Ten Eyck was knocked off the bench, which fell to the floor. Petra's support was kicked out from under her. Thanks to the block tied to her ankles, she and the Boer were more or less evenly matched in weight. They were hanged face to face on the same rope.

Reguiba pulled a hawking glove on his right hand, and whistled. His falcon fluttered down from the roof beams, alighting on his outstretched arm. He stroked the bird's head while watching the fun.

An exquisite refinement of cruelty was added after a minute had passed. The hands of the victims were cut free from their bonds, injecting the torture of hope, the hope that they might hoist themselves up and somehow relieve the suffocating pressure of the noose.

A false hope, but no less tantalizing for that.

Reguiba's men had a hilarious time savoring the death struggles, as did their master. It was the first bright spot in an otherwise dismal day of setbacks.

Much later, when the authorities finally discovered the warehouse, they were confronted with the victims of the dual hanging. By then, the lawmen were already so numbed by the violence that had previously gone down, that they hardly batted an eye at the bizarre execution.

SEVEN

Gianni Girotti's pose of world-weary sophistication was carved in stone. His many acquaintances in the jet-set world of café society knew him as a blasé idler whose most violent response to a scandal or crisis was a raised eyebrow, a tolerant smile, an eloquent shrug. His comrades in the international terror network knew him to be no less unflappable.

But when his men hustled Nick Carter into his presence, Girotti looked like he'd been goosed with a cattle prod.

His eyes bulged. His jaw dropped. A lit cigarette fell from his gaping mouth into his lap, where it scorched a hole in his expensive custom-tailored slacks. He jumped up from his chair, both in response to Carter's unexpected appearance and to the painful burn inflicted by the cigarette.

"Solano! What are you doing here?"

"Surprised to see me?" Carter said. "I shouldn't wonder."

"I thought you were dead!"

"I'm not—no thanks to you and those idiots you teamed me up with. And speaking of idiots, tell your stooge to take his gun out of my back.''

It was night, and Carter had come to Gianni Girotti's villa, an imposing structure set atop a rocky hill overlooking the town of Lulav on the bay.

Villa? Palazzo was a more accurate description. Built in the 1920s, it mingled Mediterranean and Turkish motifs in a mansion that was many-roomed, lavish, sprawling. It was surrounded by terraces, gardens, and arcades. Its grounds even boasted some ancient stone blocks, silent reminders that the villa was but a brash newcomer in this storied land.

The grounds also boasted plenty of guards, some of whom had taken Carter in hand when he strolled up the curving road rising from town. They escorted him indoors, where he was turned over to tougher, more brutal guards.

One of them, Tuttle, an American, ground the muzzle of his .357 magnum into Carter's spine as he was taken to Girotti. A mean-faced neo-Nazi from Nebraska, Tuttle fled his native land following a string of violent crimes committed in the Midwest. He ached for an excuse to hurt somebody, and Carter/Solano struck him as the likeliest candidate.

Girotti was lounging on the deck of an indoor swimming pool, located in its own separate wing. The pool was just short of Olympic size. It was illuminated by multicolored underwater lights. Chlorine-laden moisture thickened the air.

Far more spectacular than the pool was the blonde floating in it on a raft. She lounged indolently, stretched out on her belly, folded left arm pillowing her head, right arm trailing lazily in the water.

Long-legged and sleek, with a glowing tan, she wore nothing more than a shocking pink bikini bottom. Only a female with a form divine would dare to wear so minimal a costume. And this stunning female had nothing to hide—almost literally.

Her form was the only thing divine about her. She was Eva Reichenbach, and she was amoral, violent, hedonistic, and perverse. It was Eva who had provided Carter entree to Gianni Girotti's inner circle back in Milan two months ago. Girotti employed her as a "honey trap" to further his numerous schemes.

Eva stirred, lazily looking up when she heard the commotion caused by the new arrivals. When she recognized Carter at the center of the scene, her bright blue eyes went wide, narrowed, then smoldered with desire.

"Solano!"

Her cry rang in the echoing chamber. She rolled off her raft into the water and swam to the far end of the pool with swift, strong strokes.

She hoisted herself out of the pool and ran dripping across the tiles, bare feet slapping. Her short hair framed her chiseled Nordic face like a golden cap. Her tan was uniform, unbroken by any pale bikini lines. She wore no top. Her full breasts were sassily uptilted, crowned by neat dark nipples.

Carter grinned. "If you must know, she's the main reason I came back."

A snarl replaced his grin as Tuttle prodded him with the revolver.

Tuttle said, "Hey, how about you boys speakin' English so I can know what you're gabbin' about?"

"All right, Tuttle," Girotti said. "If it will make you happy. You Americans have no gift for languages."

Carter could have laughed at that one. His flawless Italian had enabled him to pass as a native for months. But Tuttle wasn't so funny. He was starting to distinctly annoy the Killmaster.

More dangerous than the clownish Nebraskan were Girotti's two personal bodyguards, the duo Carter had mentally labeled Bob and Bill.

Bill was Guillermo Lopez-Ortiz, a fine-boned Argentinian dandy who'd left the savage pampas to ply the gunman's trade on the Continent.

Bob was Roberto Martinez. Where Bill was slim and slight, Bob was a hulking physical presence, slope-shouldered and big-boned. Bob hailed from Uruguay, one of the original Tupamaros. His *compañeros* in that cause were all dead or rotting in jail, but he was still going strong on the other side of the world. His dark eyes, wide face, and high cheekbones testified that Indian blood ran in his veins.

Despite his brutish exterior, Bob was the brains of the pair. He and Bill were partners, working only as a team. A pair of dangerous professionals.

Now they flanked their boss, Girotti, who never left home without them, or stayed at home without them either. They lounged with seeming casualness, as if they couldn't have been less interested in the byplay, but they had covered Carter even before he stepped into the room.

"Solano, you beautiful bastard, I knew you were too tough to die!" Eva said. Sensing the tension, she stopped short a few paces from him. "What's wrong?"

By now, Girotti had recovered some of his savoir-faire. "We need to get a few things straightened out with our friend Solano, Eva."

She was nothing if not a survivor, knowing when to back off.

Bill and Bob were good, all right. They had to be good not to be distracted by Eva's erotic beauty. Their intent eyes never left Carter.

Staying in Solano's character, Carter blew Eva a kiss. "Keep it warm for me, baby. We've got a lot of lost time to make up for."

Eva smiled, saying nothing. She wouldn't commit

herself one way or the other until she saw which way the deal went down.

"Shut up, you!" Tuttle jabbed Carter hard. Earlier, he had grabbed Carter's arm to steer him to Girotti. It was so corded with sinewy muscle that it was like taking hold of a tree limb. But Tuttle had already forgotten about that.

"So tell us, Solano, what happened to the *Melina*?" Girotti drawled.

"Don't you watch television?"

"I want to hear it from you."

"She blew up. Those idiots on the ship must have crossed the wrong wires or something, and—*kaboom!*"

"Why didn't you blow up with it?"

"My squad had already cast off."

"You didn't blow up the oil depot," Girotti chided.

"After the explosion, the waters were crawling with patrol boats and covered with helicopters," Carter explained. "I signed on to do a job, not to commit suicide."

"And—the others in your group?"

"You know Abu-Bakir?"

"The Palestinian? I've heard of him."

"Too bad you didn't warn me about him," Carter said. "We made it to shore with no problem, but that guy didn't like the way some policemen were looking at him. He started shooting. They shot better. I was lucky. The others weren't."

"You deserted your comrades under fire?" Girotti asked silkily.

"With pleasure. You can't desert dead men, and they sure looked dead to me. I got away, stole a car, and made my way here."

Carter got mad. "Are you through playing twenty questions? It seems to me that I'm the injured party here! I signed on to do a professional job with professionals, and what do I get? A one-way ride on a ship of fools that nearly got me killed not once but often! I hold you responsible, Girotti!"

"I told you to take it easy, greaseball!" Tuttle growled.

"Where did you pick up this drugstore cowboy?" Carter asked.

"Why, you dirty—"

"That's enough, Tuttle!" Girotti barked.

"You buy that story?"

"What do you suggest?"

"Hell, it's no mystery to me!" Tuttle said. "This guy's yellow, just plain yellow, that's all! He got scared and chickened out on the job, and on his partners, too! You said it yourself—he's a damned lily-livered deserter!"

"I think not," Girotti said.

"You trust him?"

"I didn't say that, either."

"Use your head," Carter said. "I could have bought myself immunity and a fat reward by turning you all in. Instead, I came here. Maybe that was a mistake, eh?"

"It was for you, buddy boy," Tuttle snarled.

"Who's giving the orders around here, Girotti?" Carter demanded. "You, or this idiot?"

"I am," Girotti said. "Put your gun away, Tuttle."

"But—"

"I'm not asking you, I'm telling you! Put your gun down and stop baiting him!"

"Suit yourself." Tuttle sullenly obeyed.

"Sorry, but in this business, one can't be too careful. Sorry about the job, too, but, uh, these things happen. I'm glad you made it," Girotti said.

"So am I," Eva purred.

Girotti held out his hand. Carter shook it. Bob and Bill eased their intent awareness.

"My boss will want to talk to you," Girotti said.

"You know where to find me," Carter said. "Oh, yes, one thing more."

The Killmaster's right hand was a blur of light-ninglike motion as he planted a solid haymaker square on the button of Tuttle's chin.

There was the solid, satisfying thud of fist striking flesh, a click as the blow slammed Tuttle's jaws shut, and a rush of air as Tuttle backpedaled, arms windmilling. A wall interrupted his progress. He slid down and slumped to the floor, head lolling, out cold.

Carter messaged his front knuckles. "Sweet dreams, buddy boy."

Bob and Bill exchanged glances, impressed.

Carter said, "If you don't mind, I'd like to get some good food in my belly. It's been too long since I've had a decent meal. All they ever served on board ship was couscous. If I ever seen another plate of that slop again, I'll vomit."

"I think you'll find our bill of fare to your liking," Girotti said with a smile.

"Knowing your gourmet tastes, I'm sure of it. And while I'm on the subject, a bit of *vino* wouldn't hurt either."

"The wine cellar is extensive. Make yourself at home."

"Thanks, I'll do just that," Carter said.

"Ah, one thing, Solano. It would be best if you didn't try to leave the villa for now."

"With a dragnet in full swing, and me without a passport? Where would I go?"

"My sentiments exactly."

Carter slipped an arm around Eva's waist. Her satin skin was still moist from the pool.

"Solano, ummmm . . ." She leaned into him. "Long time no see."

"You don't know the half of it. I haven't so much as seen a woman for over six weeks."

"You're seeing me."

"I'll do a lot more than see," he promised.

"Then what are we waiting for?"

"Lead on, *carissima*." Arm in arm, they went to the exit. Carter paused under the archway to deliver a parting shot. "Your hired hand's got a glass jaw, Girotti."

Tuttle was still out cold. He came to after Bob and Bill tossed him in the pool.

A cordon of Israeli commandos surrounded the villa. Taking advantage of the excellent cover provided by the rugged terrain, they had moved within a few dozen yards of the structure, where they impatiently awaited the go signal. Girotti's guards, patrolling the grounds, were blissfully unaware of the camouflaged action team lurking a scant stone's throw away.

It was an Israeli operation and the AXE contingent had to take a back seat. Griff and Stanton chafed under the enforced inaction.

Hawk had told them, "Remember, we're here to observe, and that's all. Our little escapade this afternoon didn't exactly make us the most popular kids on the block. Of course, if somebody shoots at us, we can shoot back."

"That's a comfort," Griff had said. "You think this ploy will flush out the big boss, Reguiba?"

"It's worth a try."

Stanton looked long and hard at the villa. "I wonder how Nick's making out right now?"

The dinner that Girotti's chef sent up to the guest room on the second floor looked and smelled delicious. Nick Carter didn't take a bite of it. The wine accompanying it was an excellent vintage. Carter didn't drink a drop.

He didn't suspect that the food and wine were poisoned. Girotti wanted to keep him alive, at least until his boss had a chance to interrogate the sole survivor of the *Melina*. But it might well be drugged. Knocking him out would be an easy way to keep him on ice until needed. He couldn't even use Eva as an unwitting food taster, since they were perfectly capable of drugging her along with him to lend credibility to the ploy.

He couldn't eat and he couldn't drink. That left him with only one source of amusement: Eva. She was in an adjoining dressing room, having showered after her swim.

The room—suite of rooms, actually—was ornate, opulent, filled with heavy antique furniture and objets d'art. There was a crystal chandelier, a gilded oval mirror, a big bed. A bed that looked particularly inviting.

Opposite the bed, French doors opened onto a small stone balcony. Carter stepped out for a breath of fresh air.

A guard stationed on the patio below looked up. Carter flashed him a friendly wave that was neither acknowledged nor returned.

A slight motion flashed in the corner of his eye. Turning to discover its source, he saw another guard stationed on a balcony two rooms away.

He saw no sign of the Israeli action team that should have been in position by then. That was all to the good. If he couldn't see them, neither could the opposition. If he could see them, he'd really have cause for worry.

"I'll be right with you," Eva sang out.

"Good." Closing the French doors, Carter went back into the room. Eva joined him.

He whistled. *"Bellissima!"*

"You like?" she teased.

"I like."

There was plenty to like. Plenty of Eva, that is. He'd already seen her near naked tonight, so for a change of pace she'd put on something more appropriate to the bedroom, a tiny one-piece garment of black silk and lace. It tied in a halter at the back of her neck, the translucent fabric capturing her firm breasts. Its black lace hem barely reached the tops of her thighs, doing next to nothing to conceal the blond triangle between them.

Carter's hormones kicked into overdrive. It had been a long, long time. . . .

Black spike heels added inches to her already lofty height. She pirouetted, exhibiting a rear view, the cheeks of her firm buttocks only half-hidden by the teddy.

Carter applauded the total effect. Eva winced as she went to him.

"Ouch!"

"What's wrong?"

"I can hardly walk in these damned things."

"Then why wear them?"

"I like the way they look. Besides," she added, "I don't have to do much walking in bed."

"Speaking of which . . ." Carter said, embracing her. Eva made quite an armful. She had the face and figure of a high-fashion model, which she had once been before her lust for kicks and danger took her into bad company.

Her mouth was hot, sweet, devouring. Carter tasted it while his hands stroked their way down her back to her high, rounded rump. He cupped her bare buttocks under the lingerie, pulling her pelvis into his. There was a weakness in her knees as she ground her hips into his hardness.

Not breaking the rhythm of his kisses, he unknotted the halter at the back of her neck. It came undone, baring her upper body. She stroked stiff nipples against his chest, arousal writhing through her.

Suddenly she clawed the back of his neck, breaking the skin with her nails.

Fear chilled the Killmaster. He knew of an old

assassin's trick of secreting poison under the fingernails, then injecting poison into the victim's bloodstream by scratching him.

Eva's gurgling laughter reassured him that this was no insidious technique, but merely some of her kind of kinky foreplay.

"Did I hurt you, Solano? Hurt me back."

He grabbed her hair, pulled her head back, and ground his mouth to hers.

"Ummm, I like that," she murmured when they came up for air.

That cued Carter as to how to play the rest of the game. He put his hand between her bare breasts and pushed her back to the bed.

She toppled back on the bed, bouncing on its mattress, falling awkwardly so that she landed with her legs spread wide. She did not bother to close them. She placed one hand between her legs and used the other hand to beckon him to her.

Carter opened his shirt down the front but left it on. He kneeled on the bed, looming over Eva.

"Aren't you going to take your clothes off?"

"Sure," he growled. "Help me a little." And she did, and then Carter helped himself to everything the lascivious Eva had to offer.

Eva sat nude at a vanity, her bare buttocks nestled in the plush white satin cushion on the bench. She was making up her face and powdering her nose. The powder formed a little mound on a mirror. Eva leaned over it, using a cocktail straw to snort up lines.

"What's that, cocaine?" Carter asked.

"No, heroin."

"Hard to get in this country."

"Oh, Gianni can get anything. You know him." She sniffed and snuffled.

"Yes, I know him. Careful with that stuff."

"I know what I'm doing." She looked up, white powder frosting her nostrils. "Want some?"

"No, thanks. In my line of work, I can't afford to take anything which might slow me up."

Eva shrugged, then vacuumed up some more lines. When she was done, she rose, swaying a bit unsteadily. Carter held her arm, supporting her until the rush of dizziness passed.

"Whew! That stuff's pure!" Her eyes swam in and out of focus. She held on to him.

"Umm, Solano, the man they cannot kill. So tough, so hard . . . so very hard," she murmured. Her caressing hands ran over him. "Such a pleasure for a change, to be with a man who's strong and hard and knowing."

"I like you too, Eva."

"Want a replay?" she asked.

He toyed with her stiff nipples, chuckling. "Again? So soon? You're insatiable."

"I am that, but that's not what I meant." She slipped free from his embrace. "I'll show you something cute."

Eva crossed the room to a wall panel decorated with a mural of the Grand Canal in Venice. Her fingertips probed along its lower edge, tripping a concealed switch. A hidden catch sprang open with a click.

Intrigued, Carter went to it. A hairline crack, previously invisible, ran down the center of the mural, dividing it into a pair of panels that Eva now swung outward, disclosing a secret cupboard.

It was crammed with electronic equipment, the centerpiece of which was a video monitor.

"Well, I'll be a dirty—" Carter began.

"You were, darling. And still are, on tape. Here, I'll give you a peek."

Eva rewound the tape, then switched on the "play" button.

The image flickered into existence. Mirrored in tones of gray and white on the goldfish bowl of the screen was a full-length view of Carter and Eva writhing on the bed in mutual ecstasy.

"I switched on the hidden camera before we began. Like it?" Eva said.

Carter, studying the action, said, "I look pretty good in there."

"There's a setup like this in just about every room in the villa."

"I didn't know Girotti was a voyeur."

Eva laughed nastily. "To tell you the truth, Gianni's not good for much else *but* watching. But that's not why he had these installed."

"Don't tell me. I can guess. Blackmail."

"He calls it 'leverage.' It's been one nonstop party ever since we arrived. Gianni brought along a half-dozen playmates, beautiful boys and girls who are all very accommodating. We've entertained the cream of local society. Knesset politicians, industrialists from Ramat, scientists from Rehovath, Café Cassit intellectuals.

"We've been very much in demand. Everybody who's anybody wants an invitation to one of Gianni's parties. We've hosted the big men and their bored wives at bashes where the booze keeps flowing and the fun never stops. For those who want something with more of a kick than champagne, there's cocaine, hashish, pills, heroin. And plenty of beautiful young people of either sex to play with. Only once you play, you have to pay. Not with money, but with favors and obedience."

"I get the idea," Carter said. "You provide both the party and the hangover."

"That's right. Gianni's built himself up quite a little network in the short time we've been here."

"I see what I've been missing while I was stuck out on that lousy ship."

Carter jabbed the "stop" button.

"Hey! What are you doing?"

He ejected the cassette, then pulled out several dozen feet of tape, bunching them up before he tossed the mess into a wastebasket. In Carter's world, the fewer pictures of himself in existence, the better.

He made a joke out of it. "Why settle for imitations when you've got the real thing?"

Eva pouted. "Spoilsport."

A knock sounded on the door to the suite. "Yes, who is it?" Eva called out.

"It's me, Gianni. Tell Solano to get dressed and come downstairs. Somebody wants to meet him."

EIGHT

The showdown took place in what Eva called the "orgy room."

"Wait till you see it," she enthused. "It's really something! The last word in entertainment."

"I'm looking forward to it," Carter said. "I'm looking forward to meeting the big boss, too. What kind of a fellow is he?"

"I don't know. I've never met him. He's supposed to be very secretive. He meets only with Gianni. You should feel flattered that he's come out to meet you."

"I am," Carter said.

It was time to get down to brass tacks. Carter's senses were on full alert. His body vibrated with every heartbeat. His mouth was dry, his palms were moist. He looked as cool and unconcerned as if he were strolling on the Via Veneto. He concentrated on keeping his body loose, relaxed. Flexibility beats rigidity every time. When the time came, he would have to move fast.

He felt like Daniel going into the lion's den. Lion's den? Lion's mouth was more like it.

He was well equipped, however. He had brought along a pistol, expecting that it would be discovered, which it had been. Tuttle had found it and had taken it from him. But his cursory pat-down of the Killmaster had failed to detect Hugo up Carter's sleeve, not to mention Pierre, a miniature gas bomb worn high on his thigh between his legs. He'd removed his personal arsenal while Eva was in the dressing room, but everything was back in place now.

Tuttle had also overlooked Carter's communications device, but that was not surprising, since it was incorporated into the stylish wristwatch worn on his left hand. It contained a microminiatured transmitter that could be activated by pressing one of the nibs for setting the time. A pretty sophisticated piece of equipment, it even kept the correct time.

Carter was as prepared as possible.

Eva looked lovely in a sleeveless turquoise-and-white striped knit dress and high-heeled sandals. "Here we are."

"After you." Carter followed her through a door and into the "orgy room."

The large room was cleverly divided into a system of stepped terraces, forming pits, pools, alcoves, and platforms—a seductive environment of rounded forms and smooth-flowing curves with no hard edges. A scheme of indirect lighting created zones of soft, inviting light and even more invitingly intimate shadow. Banks of fragrant potted plants and shrubs partitioned the space into a maze of secluded nooks and crannies. The sweet scent of incense perfumed the air.

A death chamber for the Killmaster.

Carter knew it as soon as he entered the room. Present were Girotti, Bob and Bill, and Tuttle. No one else, no one who could be Reguiba. But that didn't mean he wasn't there. The orgy room had plenty of places in which he could conceal himself if he wished.

There was no hiding the fact that Girotti and company had tumbled to the secret of his masquerade.

Earlier they were suspicious, but they bought his story. Now they knew he was a phony. Their knowledge lurked behind a brittle facade of cool casualness.

As before, Girotti was flanked by his bodyguards, who stood with their hands resting near pistols worn in hip and shoulder holsters.

Tuttle wasn't cool. Ugly, gloating triumph marked his face, as did an enormous purple bruise from Carter's knockout punch.

"You should have killed me when you had the chance, buddy boy," Tuttle said.

"I can fix that now if you'd like," Carter retorted.

"You're the one who's gonna get fixed, wise guy."

Carter's adrenals primed his body for flight or fight.

Tuttle started toward him. "I'm gonna tear you down like a condemned building."

Girotti held up a hand. "I'm afraid you'll have to forgo that pleasure, Tuttle. Solano belongs to someone else. Or perhaps I should call him by his real name—Nick Carter."

Guns appeared in the hands of Bob and Bill. They were good, all right. Carter had hardly seen them draw, they were so fast.

Eva sidled away from Carter. She knew which way the winds were blowing, even if she lacked the big picture.

"More games?" Carter asked. "Suppose you tell me, so I can play too."

"You're good. Very good. You'd have to be good to fool me for so long. I, Gianni Girotti, salute your skill, Carter."

"The name's Solano."

Girotto shook his head. "No need to act any more, Carter. Your cover's blown. I know who you are and what you are. Or should I say what you *were*. Because as of tonight, you're done for."

Tuttle fidgeted, unable to contain himself any longer.

"I don't care if he's Jimmy Carter, I got a score to settle with that guy and I ain't kiddin'."

Girotti's eyebrows drew themselves together in a frown. "Leave us, Tuttle. You, too, Eva."

Eva was well trained. Without a word, she spun on her high heels and left the room.

"Ciao, carissima," Carter called after her.

She did not reply.

"I told you to leave, Tuttle," Girotti said.

"Nobody gives me the bum's rush."

"I won't argue, Tuttle. I'm telling you to get out while you still can."

"Sheeeyit." Tuttle reached for the revolver stuffed in his waistband.

Two shots rang out. Bob fired casually from the hip, his bullet taking off the top of Tuttle's head in a soft wet explosion of blood, brain, and bone. Bill used a more classic marksman's stance, shooting with arm extended straight out. His shot took Tuttle in the heart.

Tuttle was doubly dead.

Carter held back from making his play, even though Tuttle's death had provided an opening diversion. Girotti was enjoying his little game of cat and mouse too much to cut it short by killing Carter. Still, this waiting game was hell on the Killmaster's nerves.

Glancing at Tuttle's bloody corpse, Carter said, "Thanks. You just saved me the trouble."

"You're a cool one," Girotti said. "Let's see how cool you are when the pain begins."

"I don't know who you think I am, but you're making a big mistake—"

"It won't wash, Mr. Carter. You know a man named Tigdal?"

"Never heard of him."

"He knows you. He's my pipeline into the upper echelon of the SB's Counterforce department. Tigdal had a sister, a pretty little thing, if a bit spoiled and reckless. She came here to play, but when I found out who her brother was, why, I simply couldn't let her go. Tigdal didn't believe I had her, so I sent him a ring he'd given her for her birthday.''

Girotti paused, then delivered the punchline. ''Her finger was still attached to the ring. Since then, the lieutenant has been most cooperative.''

Carter figured Girotti for the type who could have happily gone on gloating all night long. But the arrival of his master put a halt to the game-playing.

Girotti and his bodyguards stood on a raised dais, looking down at Carter. A hairline crack appeared in the wall behind them, the leading edge of an oblong of darkness revealed when a hidden door slid back.

Reguiba stepped through it.

The trio glanced his way as he made his entrance. Carter used the opportunity to put his hand in his pocket, plunging his fingers through its slitted hole to touch Pierre. The contact was infinitely reassuring.

Reguiba stood regally, sinister in his black garments so reminiscent of the garb of the ninjas. But no ninja ever wore twin .45s holstered on his hips.

How had he managed to slip through the cordon around the villa? Carter wondered. Was he that good, or was more treachery involved?

Reguiba stared at Carter. Something odd about his eyes . . . the irises as dark as the pupils, with no line of demarcation between the two. They created the unnerving illusion of twin black holes bored through his eyeballs, a pair of gun-barrel eyes. Reguiba regarded Carter so coldly that icicles could have formed in the room.

Girotti said, unnecessarily, ''This is Carter.''

''I know,'' Reguiba said. ''He looks like the kind of man who could have sunk my ship.''

He spoke directly to Carter. "You have cost me no small trouble and expense, a debt you will repay a thousandfold."

Carter said nothing. What was there to say?

Reguiba told Girotti, "Your work here is done. The dogs are hard on your heels. Even as I speak, the hunters tighten the net around your dwelling place."

"What?"

"You will leave now, with me."

"But I can't leave just yet—"

"You must."

Girotti looked stricken. "But my work, all I've accomplished here—"

"There is work for you in Al Khobaiq. Come."

"All right, just let me get some things together."

Reguiba shook his head. "Time runs out. We must go now."

"I—" Realizing the futility of arguing with Reguiba, Girotti accepted the inevitable. He pointed at Carter. "What about him?"

"Bring him. I will exact the full measure of the blood debt he owes me."

Bob and Bill started down the stairs of the dais toward where Carter stood.

Reguiba was right. Time had run out.

The Killmaster depressed Pierre's tiny trigger button twice, a fail-safe device to prevent accidental activation. It was activated now, and this was no accident. He pulled off the special tape and it rolled down his leg and dropped to the floor, a little lead egg whose three-second safety delay was done.

Carter took a mental picture of the positions of the foursome, then squeezed his eyes shut.

He had selected his armaments well. This particular Pierre was a combination dazzle-smoke bomb, a useful tool for a one operator in the midst of his enemies.

Pierre detonated in a flash, with a loud *fizz-pop!* It

was like a gigantic flashbulb going off, a blinding glare. Even with his eyes squeezed shut, the glare was harsh, painful.

Carter threw himself to the floor. Shots rang out, none of them nearing him as he rolled sideways to Tuttle's corpse.

Clouds of choking smoke billowed from the little bomb.

Carter grabbed Tuttle's .357, jammed in the top of the dead man's pants. It was more gun than he preferred, but it would do the job and then some.

Pink and yellow afterimages danced in front of his eyes. He could imagine the blinding effect the flash must have had on those who had their eyes wide open when it went off.

Girotti and his bodyguards stumbled around like three blind mice, futilely clawing at their eyes, arms flailing, guns blasting far wide of the Killmaster.

Reguiba had better reflexes. At the instant that Pierre rolled across the floor, he had thrown himself backward, through the secret door by which he had entered.

Carter crouched on one knee, holding the gun in a two-handed grip. He squeezed off three shots.

Three shots, three kills. Gianni Girotti, Bob, and Bill spun like swivel-mounted targets in a shooting gallery. They went down, not to rise again until Judgment Day.

Carter paused to give the go signal. He hit the switch on his wristwatch, its intricate layers of wafered microchips transmitting the alert to the action team.

As if by remote control, the dull boom of concussing grenades and the typewriter chattering of automatic weapons sounded from outside the villa.

The raid was on.

Carter dashed up the dais, eyes tearing from the choking smoke fumigating the room. He ducked through the doorway in pursuit of Reguiba, flattening himself against the wall to throw off any ambush. He remembered Reguiba's twin .45s; his magnum contained at best three more shots. He would have grabbed one of the bodyguard's pistols, but the smoke had been too thick to locate the weapons.

No shots greeted him. Reguiba had taken to his heels. Carter took off after Reguiba.

He followed a long, narrow, curving corridor, dimly lit. The secret passage was a kind of companionway, snaking behind the rear walls of various rooms on the villa's ground floor. It had no side exits that Carter could see.

Reguiba had only a few seconds' head start. His soft boots muffled his footfalls, but not so much that Carter couldn't hear them.

"Oof!"

An outcry sounded ahead, where the passage ended in an open doorway. Beyond it lay a drawing room. On the floor lay one of Girotti's hired guns, a heavyset thug whom Reguiba had knocked down in the course of his mad flight.

At the opposite end of the room was another door. Carter arrived just in time to see Reguiba slam it shut behind him.

The dazed thug sat up, cleared his head, and saw Carter. He grabbed for his pistol, which lay on the floor not far from his hand.

Carter slammed him with a front snap kick, powering the ball of his foot into the fellow's jaw. He wouldn't be getting up for a while, if ever.

Carter broke stride long enough to pick up the thug's pistol. He felt better now that he was packing two guns.

He approached the closed door from the side instead of straight on. Back to the wall, he turned the door-knob.

Three slugs came crashing through the door panel at chest height. The bullet holes clustered in a tight circle, outstanding shooting with a .45.

Carter threw open the door, clearing the way with a deafening blast from the .357. There was no answering fire.

He ducked into a narrow hall no more than ten feet long. At its far end was a wide, spacious room, racketing with gunfire, none of it directed his way.

Girotti's men were making a battle of it. Two of them crouched behind overturned furniture barricaded up close to a gaping hole where a picture window used to be. They fired rifles at commandos rushing the house.

They were startled by the apparition of Reguiba loping through the room. Before they could react, he vanished around a corner.

They saw Carter, though. He dove for the floor and shot them from there.

Before he could rise, machine-gun fire from outside ripped into the room, whizzing over his head, hammering holes out of the wall in bursts of white plaster that fell like fine powdered snow.

In this fire fight, he was as much of a target for his allies as he was for his enemies.

He crawled on his belly the rest of the way out of the room, rising when he was out of the line of fire. He was in a small tiled anteroom, thick with the smell of chlorine.

Reguiba's black-clad figure darted through the wing housing the indoor swimming pool. Carter shot at him with the pistol in his left hand, and missed.

Reguiba whirled and snapped off a shot. It imploded a beautifully engraved glass panel two feet to Carter's right.

Reguiba went down a stairwell, out of sight.

Carter followed. Metal-treaded concrete stairs tilted down into a musty storeroom below the pool. The air was so oppressive that Carter could hardly draw a breath.

The vault muted the sounds of battle. A few low-watt

bulbs shed a twilight dusk over what was a kind of underground attic. Mounds of boxes, crates, and cartons were jumbled about, as well as several pieces of monumental sculpture, poor imitations of Classical statuary.

The dust was thick and that was good: it betrayed the route taken by Reguiba through the crates and curios.

Too good to be true, perhaps. Reguiba could be lurking just off the path, waiting for Carter.

Carter kept going.

Suddenly he heard a clang, like a manhole cover dropping into place. The sound was so close, Carter nearly jumped out of his skin. He continued on, scrambling in a low crouch over the tops of crates, dropping down to a clearing amidst the antique junk.

Not even the dim light could obscure the outlines of a hatchway set in the floor. In its center was an iron ring wide enough to accommodate a gripping hand.

Carter heaved open the heavy hatch.

A steep narrow flight of stone stairs dropped down to a small square chamber. The gloom cloaked Reguiba's dark body except for the pale oval of his face and his hands. He hunched over a piece of modern machinery, bent like a human question mark, making quick, furtive adjustments to what looked like switches and levers.

Firing a .45, he emptied a clip at Carter. The Killmaster was pinned down until the shooting stopped.

When Carter looked again, Reguiba was off and running.

Carter went down the stairs. The air, while thick, was moving, circulating. At the far side of the shaft, a tunnel mouth gaped. It was carved out of the living rock of the promontory. It was old, very old. Carter guessed it wormed its way through the guts of the rock to a hidden exit.

The kings of old were known to dig escape routes under their palaces and castles, and this land had been occupied since the beginning of recorded history. Who dug this tunnel? The Crusaders? The Old Testament Hebrews? The Canaanites? Or some even more ancient people?

No wonder Reguiba was able to slip through the cordon at will!

The fact that the tunnel was not the scene of a mass exodus by Girotti's cohorts proved that its existence was a closely held secret.

The square metal box bolted to the wall beside the stairs was as new as the tunnel was old. It looked not unlike a fuse box, but the fuse it contained was no circuit breaker; it was an arming device. Metal-sheathed cable sprouted from it, running vertically up the wall to disappear through a hole bored in the ceiling. Unless Carter missed his guess, the unseen end of the cable terminated in a load of explosives.

The switch inside the box was thrown to the ON position.

A delayed reaction—but how long? A second? Ten seconds? As much as a minute? It couldn't be more than a minute, Carter figured, and he wasn't going to stick around to find out.

He did what he could. He threw the switch back to OFF, grabbed the metal-sheathed cable, and tore at it. It was too tough to break with his bare hands. He doubted Hugo could saw through it. He shot it in two, recoiling from a ricochet that came dangerously close, making a crater in the rock wall not far from him.

It might be too late to stop the machine, but at least he had tried. He breathed a silent prayer of thanks that Hawk and the AXE men had been relegated to a back seat for this show.

And Eva? She would just have to take her chances.

Carter went into the tunnel after Reguiba.

It sloped downward at a fairly steep angle. The ramp did not go straight down, but made a right-angled turn every forty feet, describing a corkscrew shape as it wound its way downward.

Rubber-insulated power lines were strung along the low ceiling, held in place by metal staples, supplying current to the dim bare bulbs jutting from metal sockets at irregular intervals. There was barely enough light to see by.

Carter went down sideways, in a basketball player's stance, presenting the smallest target profile. The side stance was murder on the thigh muscles, but provided good maneuverability.

The walls glided past. The neatly square-cut section of the tunnel played out, replaced by a still older excavation crudely gouged from the rock. The walls pressed inward, narrowing, the ceiling dropping until he had to take care not to dash his brains out against low-hanging knobs.

The lights were fewer and far between, causing him to traverse long stretches in near darkness. Carter felt as if he were creeping through some giant intestine of stone.

Abruptly, that stone intestine quivered.

The explosives armed by the switch reached criticality. The villa on the bay destructed like a volcano blowing its top.

Even here, with dozens of feet of stone serving as a buffer, the impact was considerable. Carter was knocked to the floor as the lights went out.

The image of Eva, lovely Eva being obliterated in the blast flashed through Carter's being with a wrenching pang. Maybe she deserved her fate, but . . . .

A few heartbeats later, Carter was galvanized by a choking cloud of dust and debris that gusted over him. On hands and knees, his pistol hopelessly lost, he crawled forward, following the downward slope.

It would be a hell of a note for him to get this far, only to be asphyxiated in a rocky tomb, he thought grimly.

He hadn't gone far when the floor leveled off, then began to rise. Air currents played over him. The dust clouds kept coming, but he was able to breathe.

And there was light of a sort, the faintest luminescence ahead.

Carter kept low. If Reguiba launched a bullet in his direction, it would pass overhead.

There was the click of a spring and the soft slap of Hugo's hilt sliding into his open palm. The long stiletto was a divining rod seeking not water, but blood.

The blood of Reguiba.

The tunnel ended in a cleft in the base of the hill which turned sharply right, then left. Fresh air revitalized him, making him aware of how much the fine-grained choking grit had filled his lungs, the very pores of his skin.

Carter worked his way through a thicket of tight-packed, thorny scrub, and eventually emerged on the apron of dirt and loose stones at the base of the hill.

He was on the north face of the rock knob, lonely and desolate terrain. The promontory's bulk stood between him and the city lights of Lulav, but he could see well enough. Firelight from the burning villa shed red glare and macabre shadows on the lower slopes.

There was nothing for Carter to do but watch the fire.

Reguiba had made his escape.

The Killmaster had crossed paths with a master killer.

NINE

The next day found Nick Carter en route to the quasi-independent emirate of Al Khobaiq, Saudi Arabia. He had plenty to think about during the flight.

Bar-Zohar's SB action team had one dead, two critically wounded, and a number of minor injuries. Only the stiff resistance offered by Girotti's men kept the Israeli body count as low as it was. The villa's defenders held the attackers at bay right up until the all-consuming explosion.

The self-destruct mechanism demonstrated that Reguiba was a man who tied up loose ends. It had probably been installed to serve as a surprise ending to one of Girotti's famous parties, wiping out a crowd of important and influential guests at one stroke. Faking his own death, Girotti then could have surfaced with a new identity.

Instead, Reguiba used the hellish setup to wipe the slate clean. Only two survivors were pulled from the smoking rubble, and they were what Eva had called "playmates," sexual lures, mere pawns holding no important information.

The night produced one more casualty, Lieutenant

Avi Tigdal, who shot himself in the head less than one minute after the villa blew. A confession was found among his personal effects, a tragic account of how he had been forced into treason in the vain hope of saving his sister. Deborah Tigdal was never seen again, and was presumed dead.

Carter underwent an intensive debriefing session lasting well into dawn. Thanks to his description, an identikit portrait of Reguiba was constructed, the first time that his likeness had ever been captured. Capturing the likeness was easy compared to capturing the man, but thousands of copies of the composite image were circulated to every police and military unit in Israel.

Reguiba was the object of one of the most extensive manhunts in the nation's history. A small army of searchers all but turned the country upside down, but they came up empty-handed.

"There's every reason to believe that he's left the country as easily and undetected as he entered it," Bar-Zohar said. "This man moves across international boundaries as if they didn't exist."

His investigators managed to dig up the first piece of solid information relating to Reguiba. Early in the morning, a grizzled old man named Salahuddin Yizkorou—"Salah"—was brought to Shin Bet headquarters to tell his story. A translator rendered his Hebrew into English for the benefit of the AXE men.

Salah was a Moroccan Jew who had lived an adventurous life, spending a good part of it serving in the military police in the southern desert not far from the Mauritanian border. It was a harsh, forbidding land of mountains and bone-dry, flinty plains infrequently broken by oases and water holes. No less rugged were its people, nomadic tribes who still lived by the age-old traditions of raiding and blood feuds.

Most feared among the desert dwellers were the tribes of the Reguibat. Their uneasy neighbors had a saying:

"The Reguibat is a black cloud over the sun." This referred not only to the tribal custom of wearing all-black garb, but also to their prowess in the arts of raiding, robbery, and murder.

The last post held by Salah before retiring from the service some twenty years ago was in the town of Goulimine, where the Reguibat came to trade. Here he heard a curious story.

A clan of the haughty Yaqbah Reguibat banished a young warrior for violating some sacred taboo. This nameless youth's unknown crime was so grievous that the tribal elders had him shorn of his manhood, that his seed would not spawn to pollute the earth.

The mutilated youth abandoned the desert for the cities, where he quickly made a name for himself as an enforcer and assassin for slave and drug syndicates. He was known only as "the Reguiba," or simply "Reguiba," the singular of the tribal name. He was a most singular character.

Feral and fearless, in no time at all he had shot his way to the top of the Moroccan underworld. Little more was known about him save that secrecy, falconry, and murder were his ruling passions.

As for the clan that had castrated and expelled him, they had ceased to exist. Most of the males died in a single night, victims of a mass poisoning at a banquet. Nor were the women and children spared. One by one, they were rooted out and exterminated by a relentless stalker, until only Reguiba remained alive of all his clan.

"There is work for you in Al Khobaiq."

That was one of the last things Reguiba had said to Girotti. It meant there was work there for the Killmaster, too.

A U.S. Air Force jet could have delivered him quickly to the emirate, but it would have attracted too much attention. No commercial flights were available on a direct route from Israel to Saudi Arabia. A quick hop by helicopter delivered Carter to Beirut International Airport, where he caught a jet to his destination on the Persian Gulf.

He was not traveling alone. With him was the 9mm antidote to the Reguiba problem, his trusted companion of countless missions, Wilhelmina.

Hawk surprised Carter with the Luger while seeing him off at the airport. "This package was just delivered by special courier, Nick. I sent for it when you turned up like the proverbial bad penny."

The package contained Wilhelmina holstered in a fast-draw holster rig. Carter did not bother to hide his pleasure as he hefted the precision-tooled pistol, savoring its solid weight and satisfying balance.

"Thanks, sir. Thanks a lot."

"I'm sure you'll put it to good use."

"You can depend on that," Carter said.

With a foul-smelling black cigar wedged in the corner of his mouth, laying down a literal smoke screen, Hawk was in an expansive mood.

"Back in the thirties, before your time, a hoodlum named Lepke got the bright idea of specializing in murder. He formed a mob of hit men dealing exclusively in assassinations for the national crime syndicate, an outfit called Murder, Incorporated."

"I've heard of it," Carter said.

"Reguiba's come up with a modern variation on that classic theme. He's put terrorism on a businesslike basis. Call it Terror, Incorporated."

Carter smiled thinly. "As I recall, Lepke ended up frying in the electric chair. I don't have one of those, but I'll put plenty of heat on Reguiba."

Hawk expected no less. "There's every possibility that Reguiba is conducting an action in the emirate, as part of Operation Ifrit. Hodler's presence there would seem to confirm it."

Karl Kurt Hodler was East German, a blond giant, a former Olympic athlete turned liquidator. A one-man mob. Hodler had worked in conjunction with Girotti in northern Italy, spearheading a wave of kidnappings, kneecappings, and killings.

"I'll smoke out Reguiba through Hodler," Carter said.

"You'd do well to keep in mind that our man in Al Khobaiq dropped off the board shortly after sighting Hodler. Don't underestimate the East German. You'll have your hands full with him even if Reguiba doesn't show up."

"I think he will, sir, especially when he finds out that I'm on the scene. I've given him a bloody nose, and Reguiba isn't the type to let bygones be bygones."

"That's the plan, Nick. You're live bait. You're one of the few who've seen Reguiba's face and lived to tell the tale," Hawk said. "At least you won't be working entirely on your own. Emir Bandar is cooperating a hundred percent with us. Apparently he's not too fond of the idea that a gang of thugs is plotting to steal his kingdom out from under him.

"Your local contact is Prince Hasan. From what I've heard, he's quite a character. Bon vivant, racing car enthusiast, ladies' man."

"Sounds like we have a lot in common," Carter said with a grin.

"Except that he's a member of one of the richest families in the world, while you're on an expense account," Hawk growled. "So try to keep the expenditures within reason, okay?"

"I'll do my best, sir."

A specially designed and AXE-made attaché case allowed Carter to board the plane in Beirut with his *ménage à trois* of Hugo, Pierre, and Wilhelmina. He'd put the trio on his person once he landed. He was freshly showered, clean-shaven, outfitted in clean new clothes, and had even had time to get a trim at the airport barber shop.

A pretty flight attendant turned her warm dark eyes his way, but Carter was too bushed to do more than a little casual flirting. He dozed for a good part of the flight, catching up on his rest.

He awoke for the last leg of the trip, as the jet made its final approach. The tiny, oil-rich emirate lay on the east coast of the Arabian boot, located midway between the Shatt-al-'Arab and the Strait of Hormuz, bordering the province of Hasa.

The seemingly endless expanse of sun-baked land gave way first to the coastal marshes, then to the silver-blue Persian Gulf.

The plane swooped in for a landing at one of the many runways at Dharbar Terminal, which petrodollars had transformed into one of the most modern and extensive facilities of its kind in the world. Limitless blue space became bounded by the horizon as the jet touched down, the landing gear contacting the tarmac with a bump and a squeal.

As he prepared to disembark, Carter recalled the last thing old Salah had said. He had quoted another old desert proverb:

"Should you meet a cobra and a Reguiba, spare the cobra."

"Welcome to Al Khobaiq, Mr. Fletcher. I'm Wooten. Greer sent me to drive you into town."

"Pleased to meet you," Carter said.

This time out, he was under light cover, posing as one Lewis Fletcher and carrying ID to match. His papers identified him as a high-ranking CIA official to whom every assistance would be rendered. He outranked Greer, who was the Company's representative in Al Khobaiq. Only the CIA's Director of Operations and a handful of his most trusted aides knew that AXE used their agency to provide cover for agents on special assignment, such as Carter.

They weren't happy about that use, but they accepted it as one of the unfortunate facts of life in the current political climate. The difference between the CIA and AXE was like the difference between a big-city police department with its thousands of employees, and a SWAT team.

AXE was no intelligence collector, though that was part of its mission. AXE was an enforcement arm, carrying out the covert activities that the CIA could no longer undertake. The CIA was a sieve, leaking like crazy.

In all fairness, Carter often wondered how enthusiastic he would be about carrying out his assignments if he, like his CIA counterparts, had to worry about his actions being the stuff of congressional hearings and front-page headlines at some future date.

Therefore, he was Lewis Fletcher, CIA, for as long as the guise proved useful.

Carter bypassed customs courtesy of Emir Bandar al Jalubi, the absolute ruler of the tiny state, whose servitors had arranged for the Killmaster to be waved through the time-consuming red tape afflicting ordinary visitors. Emir Bandar liked to think of himself as all-powerful, but if he really were, he wouldn't be sweating the threat of Reguiba.

This was Carter's first visit to Al Khobaiq, though it was far from his first encounter with the Arabian peninsula. Technically, the emirate was independent of, though closely allied to, the House of Saud, but they shared an identical culture. It was a strange land to a Westerner, a puritannical land where customs officials tore out photographs of bikinied beauties in American news magazines, yet where executions by beheading were broadcast live on state-controlled television. Like other sexually repressed cultures, it seethed with torrid passions that could boil over into outbreaks of frightful violence.

Carter met Wooten under a big sign proclaiming in English and Arabic: WARNING! DRUG SMUGGLERS WILL BE EXECUTED!

Wooten was in his mid-forties, big, beefy, red-haired, broad-shouldered. He wore a sweat-stained khaki shirt and slacks, red bandanna, and thick-soled boots.

They shook hands. Carter typed Wooten as a macho man who'd put all other males to the test, so he was braced when Wooten tried to apply a bone-crushing grip.

Wooten felt as if he'd caught his hand in a hydraulic press. Carter continued smiling blandly as he applied the pressure, making the burly man squirm. Past experience had taught him that it was best to establish his dominance at the start with Wooten's type of aggressive he-man. When he thought the lesson had been learned, he let go of Wooten's hand, now red and throbbing.

"No, don't bother, I'll carry my own bag, thanks," Carter said.

Wooten hadn't offered; it was just Carter's way of giving him the needle.

"Quite a grip you've got there," Wooten said. When Carter wasn't looking, he flexed his numb hand to restore its circulation.

Suitcase in hand, Carter followed Wooten across the broad expanse of the terminal, out the front doors. It was like stepping into an oven.

Now it was Wooten's turn to grin. "Mild day. Shouldn't reach more than a hundred degrees in the shade. Of course, there's no shade to speak of."

Carter wore a lightweight safari-style jacket, openneck short-sleeved shirt, loose-fitting tan trousers, cotton socks, and desert boots. When he stepped into the sun, it was almost like a physical blow. At least his tropical clothes would trap the sweat and keep it from evaporating too fast. Dehydration and heatstroke could easily afflict an unacclimatized man, and not even the hot sun of the Mediterranean could prepare a man for this heat.

Not to mention the fact that the safari jacket hid Wilhelmina in her shoulder harness.

The car was a long pearl-gray limo with tinted windows. Making a show of service, Wooten opened the rear door for Carter. "Your chariot awaits."

Carter tossed his suitcase in the back, then went to the front door on the passenger side. "The Arabs reserve the back seat for their womenfolk, I believe. The men always sit up in front."

"Right you are, mate. But we're not Arabs."

"Still, I wouldn't want to lose face among the locals." Carter climbed in the front seat.

Wooten slammed the back door. "Anything you say, Fletcher. You're the boss. That's what Greer told me, anyhow." He got behind the wheel, started the car, and drove off.

An eight-lane superhighway connected Dharbar Terminal to the seaport city of Al Khobaiq, the provincial capital and only real city of note. The impressively engineered ribbon of road had little traffic to speak of. A fraction of the population owned cars, but those few who did drove big twelve- and sixteen-cylinder tanks like the limo. It took a mighty motor to power a heavy vehicle with the air conditioner roaring at full blast.

The only speed limit was how fast a car could go. Wooten took brutal pleasure in manhandling the machine at high speeds over the roadway's long, banked curves. If he thought to make Carter nervous enough to request that he please slow down, he was crazy. The Killmaster was in a hurry himself.

The roadside was dotted with the burnt-out, ruined wrecks of crashed cars. "The Khobaiquis haven't quite gotten the hang of safe driving yet,'' Wooten said and grinned.

Nearing the city, they passed shapeless, black-clad figures, barefoot females leading mules and camels. In a land that jealously guarded its females, women were completely veiled.

They rolled through the rugged mountain ranges west of the city, which served to trap moisture blown in from the Gulf, accounting for the pale green scrub of the coast. Between the ridge and the city, the plain was covered by a sprawling shantytown, looking like a collage made from bits of rubbish, teeming with the desperately impoverished.

There was a potential trouble spot for the Emir, thought Carter. One of many.

Then they were in sight of the Gulf and the city fronting it, a city that had existed since the days of the frankincense trade over two thousand years ago.

Al Khobaiq looked like an illustration from *Tales of the Arabian Nights*. A dazzling cluster of white cubes, bristling with spiked domes and minaret spires. A cat's-cradle of telephone and power lines threaded the seaport.

A closer approach revealed the intricate detailing of broad market squares, souks, bazaars with countless tented booths offering their wares. If you wanted to look for Aladdin's lamp, that was the place to do it, thought Carter.

The harbor was crowded with boats of all types, from oil tankers to dhows, with their graceful triangular lateen sails, unchanged since the days when Sinbad set forth on his legendary voyages.

A closemouthed man, Wooten unbent enough to allow, "Quite a sight, huh, Fletcher?"

"Quite."

Unlike CIA men in mellower political climes, Greer

was not attached to the U.S. embassy in Al Khobaiq. Ever since the original Iranian hostage crisis, the word had gone out to Islamic radicals that a sure source of American spies could be found at the local diplomatic mission.

Greer's cover job was a suitably vague position with a dealership supplying pricey consumer goods to wealthy Arabs and the PXs and commissaries operating in Petro Town near the oil fields.

Greer's office was located in the newly built business and governmental district north of the city proper, planted on a hillside some distance from the waterfront.

"The air's a whole hell of a lot cleaner up here," Wooten said. "You get the sea breezes but not the stink of the city."

The hilltop had been flattened and covered with concrete. Rising around the central square was a collection of modernistic office buildings that would have looked at home in any industrial park in the world. Surrounding them were parking lots crammed with cars, few of them American-made, Carter noted.

The construction was new, but it showed much pitting from wind-blown sand scouring the surfaces. Greer's office windows were sand-blasted to near opacity, spoiling what otherwise would have been a spectacular fourteenth-floor view of the city.

The office was standard issue. There was the same desk and furniture, lighting, neutral pastel walls, and mediocre abstract art that Carter had seen in scores of similar offices worldwide.

Greer was in his mid-thirties, with thinning brown hair, a round pink face, and a trim sandy mustache. He met with Carter while Wooten cooled his heels in the outer reception area.

After the ritualized formality of exchanging recognition codes, Greer said, "You're a heavy hitter, Mr. Fletcher."

"What makes you say that?" Carter asked.

"One of the emir's people called, asking if there was anything they could do to expedite your mission. Very impressive! I've been here for over eighteen months now, and I can't even get the undersecretary to the vizier to return my phone calls. By the way, he didn't say just what your mission is."

"Then I won't either," Carter said.

Greer was not offended. "All very hush-hush, hmmm? Fine. In that case, I'll ask no questions so you won't have to tell me any lies. Regional Control says I'm to extend full cooperation. You must rate pretty high in the Company, too. So, what can I do for you?"

"I'd like to talk to Howard Sale, please," Carter said.

Greer looked blank. "Who?"

"Howard Sale. He's the local dealer for Securitron. He supplied the security system for this layout."

"Oh, you mean Howie!" Greer smiled. "Sure, I know Howie! It just took me a minute to connect the name with the face. Howie Sale, sure! He's a green kid, but I like him. Haven't seen him since the fire."

"What fire?"

"There was a pretty bad fire in his office last week," Greer said. "I haven't seen Howie since then, so I thought he got recalled home by the Company. I don't mind telling you, it made me nervous. The fire, that is. I hope the system he installed in here doesn't short out and burn the place down."

"I'd really like to get hold of Howard Sale. Do you have his office address?"

"Sure. You won't have to go far, either. It's right across the square."

"I'd also like his home address. And the names of any of his friends and associates."

"Can't help you on that last," Greer said. "Howie's a one-man operation, and he held down that office by himself. As for who his friends might be, that's a mystery to me.''

"Maybe you could ask around.''

"I'll do that. As for his home address, I know he had bachelor quarters over in Petro Town. I can give them a call over there and nail it down for you if you'd like.''

"I'd like,'' Carter said.

TEN

Carter paused at a pay phone in the lobby.

"You could have called for free from Greer's office," Wooten said.

"I'm trying to save the taxpayers a little money."

"Or maybe you didn't want Greer to listen in on the extension." Wooten hovered at Carter's back, craning his neck to see what number the Killmaster was calling.

"You don't mind if I make this a private call, do you?" Carter growled.

"Top-secret stuff, huh?" Wooten said. "Suit yourself." Shrugging, he shuffled a few paces away. "Lotsa luck on making your connection. The phone service isn't so hot around here."

Wooten was right. Working from memory, Carter punched the number Hawk had given him. Five frustrating minutes later, when he was half convinced that his memory might not be so hot anymore, he connected with Prince Hasan's answering service. Carter began in Arabic, but the voice on the other end of the line replied in English.

Prince Hasan was out of the city and temporarily unavailable, but if the caller would leave a message stating where he could be reached, the prince would contact him at the earliest opportunity.

Carter gave his Lewis Fletcher name and said he could be reached after six in the evening at the Grand Sojourn Hotel.

With Wooten in tow, he crossed the square to the building housing Howard Sale's office.

The Securitron office was a burnt-out suite of gutted, fire-blackened rooms. The smell of charred debris still hung in the air, a week later. Plywood panels were nailed up where the doors used to be in a makeshift attempt to seal off the rooms. A quick peek through a chink in the barrier was enough to determine that everything inside was totally destroyed.

That made Carter feel a bit better.

The short-lived, high-intensity fire had sizzled Securitron to a meltdown, while barely touching the neighboring offices.

"That's suspicious as hell, if you ask me," Wooten said. "I make it arson."

He was right, but not in the sense he meant. Howard Sale was an AXE operative, a field agent whose cover was as a local representative of Securitron, selling electronic security devices. There really was a Securitron, home-based in Lowell, Massachusetts. It was an AXE proprietary company, whose real business was producing high-resolution cameras for orbiting spy satellites. The research was so hush-hush that no civilian company could enforce the needed security measures. Therefore, AXE owned the company outright. Securitron also marketed a line of burglar alarms and smoke detectors as a sideline, to camouflage the company's true purpose.

The office had been destroyed not by an arsonist, but by an arson machine, a last-ditch self-destruct mechanism linked to sophisticated computer terminals on the premises. Some unauthorized person had tried to access the computer memory banks without the correct password codes and entry keys, triggering the white-hot incandescent blaze that left the machinery so much useless slag, as well as burning up the office.

"I've seen all there is to see around here," Carter said. "Let's go."

"Where to?" Wooten asked.

"Petro Town."

The man-made oasis of Petro Town stood some twenty miles northwest of the city. Getting there was no problem. The emirate had one of the best highway systems the Killmaster had ever encountered, and traffic was light.

Petro Town rose within sight of the southern rim of the Zubeir Depression, one of the most oil-saturated places on the planet. A handful of pumps stood sentinel along the perimeter.

Support personnel are required to operate a field of that magnitude—engineers and administrators, mechanics, drivers, loaders, pipe fitters, hydraulics experts, geologists, and many others. The majority of the technologically sophisticated staff had to be imported from overseas.

Petro Town existed to house and serve them. It was a startling slice of Americana set down in the desert, an enclave of over thirty-five hundred souls. Its layout was similar to military posts in other parts of the world, and it boasted all the comforts and conveniences of home: a giant PX, schools, churches, two movie theaters, even a bowling alley.

Here, security was a concept, not a reality. Carter winced at the site's aching vulnerability, the sketchiness of the fence surrounding it, the lackadaisical good humor of the hot, tired, bored guards, few in number.

He hated to think of what a suicidal car bomber could do here, or the havoc a few well-placed rockets could wreak. What a prime target!

A gate guard directed Carter and Wooten to Howard Sale's residence. While not an oil man, Sale lived in Petro Town to be among his countrymen.

He lived in a small, neat, flat-roofed bungalow fronted by a square of parched lawn in a section relegated to the bachelors. A tract on the other side of the avenue held the family men with their wives and children. After Al Khobaiq, where the few females abroad were wrapped and veiled in the traditional *chador*, it was a bit of a thrill to see women and girls openly strolling about clad in halters and shorts and slacks.

Superintending the bachelor quarters was a transplanted American couple, Gus and Millie Ferguson. He was a former oil field roughneck who had semiretired into this maintenance job. He had a gray crew cut and a belly that said that here was a man who bought his beer not by the sixpack, but by the case. Millie was fleshy, flushed, sweaty, and irritable at having to come out in the heat of the day to let Carter and Wooten into Howard Sale's quarters.

"Don't rightly know as I should let you in," Millie said, fumbling with her ring of keys. "What with Mr. Sale not being here, I mean."

"That's why we're here, Mrs. Ferguson," Carter said. "We're a bit worried about Howard. His folks haven't heard from him for some time. I'm sure you'll be happy to help out."

"Well, when you put it that way . . ."

"I been a little concerned about the kid myself," Ferguson said.

"Why is that, Mr. Ferguson?"

"Call me Gus."

"Glad to," Carter said. "You've been worried about him, you said?"

"Yeah. He always struck me as a decent sort—nice, quiet, regular hours. You know. But in the last few weeks, he changed. Stayed away for days at a time, came in at midnight only to go right back out again. That sort of thing."

Millie sniffed. "I didn't care for the company he was keeping. There was one fellow who came here a few times, a fancy-talking Ay-rab I didn't cotton to."

"Would you recognize him if you saw him again?" Carter asked.

"Land sakes, no! I can't tell one of 'em apart from the other!"

"You couldn't forget that slick car of his," Ferguson said. "Big red sports car, looking more like a goddamned spaceship than an automobile."

When Millie turned the doorknob to fit the key in the lock, the door opened. "Well, that's funny! It wasn't locked. I hope nobody took anything."

"Much theft around here?" Carter asked.

"Just from the whites," Ferguson said. "The Arabs don't steal nothing. Penalty for stealing is to get their hand chopped off."

"That would be a deterrent."

Millie said, "If anything's missing, we're not responsible for it. We can't go around checking doors to make sure they're locked."

"No reason why you should be liable," Carter said equably.

They went in. Howard Sale was neat, especially for a bachelor. A quick once-over failed to turn up anything of importance.

Set on top of a bureau was a framed photo. Carter recognized Sale from other photos shown him by Hawk. Sale was young, and looked serious, sincere, earnest.

Pictures and faces can lie; Carter's instincts told him this one didn't. The picture showed Sale with his arm around a plain, sweet-faced girl.

A wall calendar furnished a poignant note. It was decorated with a scene of an Alpine landscape. Sale had made what they used to call in the service a "short-timer's calendar," marking off with red X's the days of the month. The X's ended in the middle of the previous week, right about the time Sale notified AXE that Hodler was in the area.

After a little more poking around, Carter said, "We're through here. Thanks."

They exited, Carter and Wooten first, the Fergusons lingering to lock up. Carter whispered to Wooten, "Somebody searched the place before us."

"Yeah, I noticed that, too," Wooten said.

Gus Ferguson muttered an oath. "The door won't lock. It's busted."

Behind the row of houses were modular units with sliding overhead doors. "What're those?" Carter asked.

"Garages," Ferguson said. "The sun and the wind plays hell on a car's finish. Sand gets in the engine, fouls it up . . ."

"Does Sale have one?"

"Sure, right behind his house."

"Let's have a look," Carter said.

The garage door was rolled down, locked. Carter smelled trouble . . . and something else.

After some searching, Ferguson found the correct key. Making a show of the effort it cost him, he unlocked the door and rolled it up. "What the hell . . . !"

Millie held her nose and fanned the air in front of her face. "Whew! It stinks in here!"

The interior was a simmering cube of brown meat. It held no car, only the single surrealistic note of a fifty-gallon oil drum. Its sides and the floor around it were covered with black stains.

"Dang!" Gus said. "You can never get that stuff out!"

Carter found a tire iron on a worktable against the wall and held it out toward Wooten. "How about opening that up?"

"Why don't you?"

"Because I'm in charge."

"Thanks a lot, pal." Wooten went to the barrel, nose crinkling in disgust. "Smells kind of ripe."

"Yes," Carter said.

Ferguson shook his head. "I thought that kid had more sense than that. What does he need a barrel of oil for? That's like selling ice to the Eskimos!"

"Maybe Sale didn't put it there," Carter said. "Maybe somebody else did."

"Huh? Why would anybody want to pull a damn fool stunt like that? Some kind of practical joke?"

The drum top was sealed with a metal snap-on lid. Wooten worked the wedge of the tire from under it. "Shit! I just got some on my pants!"

"Send the cleaning bill to Greer," Carter said. "Open it up."

"That'll make a terrible mess," Millie said.

"We'll be happy to take care of any expenses, ma'am."

The lid opened with a popping noise as it was pried off.

A hideous stench poured out of it. Gagging, Wooten levered off the lid, which fell with a clang on the floor.

A hand clapped over his mouth and nose, Wooten backed off from the barrel. Carter took the tire iron from him, held his breath, and poked around at the thing floating in the barrel.

The oil was just a preservative. A human figure was stuffed in the barrel in the fetal position, the top of his oil-saturated head bobbing and drifting.

"Holy Hannah!" Ferguson breathed. "What—what's that?!"

"I wouldn't be surprised if it's Howard Sale," Carter said.

Millie Ferguson's shriek died out before it could reach any real volume. She fell to the floor in a faint.

Making a positive identification of the corpse wouldn't be easy. Carter's quick inspection revealed that the head was minus its ears, nose, and lips. He had little doubt that other parts of its anatomy were similarly excised. And he had no doubt at all that the victim of torture and murder was Howard Sale.

Carter wondered if Sale had taken any consolation in having the last laugh on his tormentors. He took the secret of the auto-incendiary device to his grave, preventing his killers from cracking into AXE's computerized communications network.

Sale would be avenged. That would provide scant comfort for the dead man, but it would give a great deal of satisfaction to the Killmaster.

"But why put the poor guy in a barrel of oil?" Greer wanted to know when Carter met with him back in Al Khobaiq. "And why hide him in his garage, of all places?"

"Somebody's got a twisted sense of humor. And he was meant to be found. Call it a psychological warfare ploy. Kill one, terrify a hundred."

Greer shook his head. "Rough stuff. Who'd do a thing like that?"

"That's what I'm trying to find out," Carter said. With Tigdal's treachery fresh in his mind, Carter hadn't taken Greer into his confidence. He felt safer playing a lone hand. "Have you got anything for me?"

"I came up with something you might find useful. According to my sources, Sale's been a regular at the

Crescent Club during the last few weeks.''

"The Crescent Club? What's that?"

"I'm surprised Wooten hasn't mentioned it to you. He's rather fond of it himself. You see, the Khobaiqis are a lot like us Americans—they're hypocrites. They have laws forbidding just about everything under the sun, but somehow there's always a way to get around them.

"Khobaiqi nightlife is a contradiction in terms, with the happy exception of the Crescent Club. If you want to gamble, drink, or womanize, the Crescent Club's the only game in town. It's a place where just about anything goes, so long as you can pay for it.''

"Sounds promising," Carter said. "I'd like to have a look at it.''

"I don't doubt it," Greer said.

"How do I get there?"

"It's about ten miles away, on the southern highway," Greer said. "Wooten knows how to get there. He can drive you out there tonight.''

"Good.''

"How are you getting along with Wooten, by the way? He can be cantankerous at times.''

"Oh, I think we understand each other," Carter said.

"Fine. One bit of advice—watch your step at the club. It's frequented by some pretty rough characters.''

"You've been there?"

"But of course," Greer said, grinning. "Khobaiqi or foreigner, anybody who's looking for a good time turns up at the Crescent Club. Like I said, it's the only game in town.''

Prominently mentioned in Karl Kurt Hodler's dossier was his virtual addiction to the pleasures of the flesh. Hodler craved his wine, women, and song. The pattern was all starting to come together . . .

"See you later," Carter said with a wave.

• • •

The Grand Sojourn Hotel was new. Except for the city's Old Quarter, everything in Al Khobaiq seemed to have been built in the last twenty years, the product of enormous oil revenues.

Carter turned his evening clothes over to the hotel staff for pressing. He took a dip in the indoor pool, knocking out a half-mile's worth of laps. Refreshing though it was, the swim failed to wash out the haunting image of Howard Sale in a barrel.

At least the exercise broke some of the tension. Carter felt loose, flexible, and able to absorb whatever the evening might bring.

He dined alone on indifferent French cuisine in the hotel restaurant. Returning to his room, he discovered that the simple detectors he'd left in place were untampered with, indicating that there had been no unauthorized entry.

The bellboy returned with his formal wear. Carter wore a white dinner jacket, black tie, black slacks, and the unholy trio of Hugo, Wilhelmina, and Pierre.

On his way out, he stopped by the desk to see if there were any messages for Lewis Fletcher. Prince Hasan had not yet returned his call.

Carter's vanity was pleased by the figure his image cut in the lobby's mirrored walls. Wooten was waiting for him, leaning against the pearl-gray limo parked by the front entrance.

He chuckled. "You look like a headwaiter in that getup."

Carter let the remark pass. He noted a bulging lump under Wooten's sloppy sport shirt, indicating the presence of a gun.

Carter needn't have worried about being overdressed. Night had come, and as in other desert climes, the temperature had dropped dramatically, by some thirty degrees or more, since the sun had gone down. It was even a bit brisk.

The car exited the hotel's horseshoe-shaped drive to pick up the southern highway. To the right rose the hills; to the left a swollen orange half-moon rose out of the sea above the city. The highway was a smooth silver ribbon rolling through a bleakly spectacular lunar landscape.

No more than five minutes had passed before Wooten said, "We've got a tail."

Having noted a pair of reflected headlights bobbing in the rearview mirror, Carter was not surprised. "Turn off at the next road you come to. Let's make sure they're really following us, and not just going south."

"Right, boss."

"I thought Greer was your boss."

"You outrank him. If I play my cards right, maybe you can fix it so that I'm his boss."

"You never can tell," Carter said.

Wooten swung right, entering a two-lane blacktop road running west and rising up a long, gently sloping hill. "They're still coming."

"Speed up."

The trailing car speeded up too. "They're gaining on us—fast," Wooten said. "Don't worry, I'll lose 'em!"

On a long straightaway, Wooten pulled what is known as the "bootlegger's turn" south of the Mason-Dixon line. Not slowing, he stomped the emergency brake while hauling the wheel hard left.

Tires howled as the car executed the ultimate in controlled skids, pivoting into a 180-degree turn that pointed its nose in the opposite direction.

Carter felt as if he'd left his stomach a hundred yards back. Wooten pulled the emergency brake and tromped the accelerator. The car shot forward, heading for a straight-on collision with the pursuer. Wooten leaned on the horn, adding to the confusion.

The pursuit car wheeled hard right to avoid a crash. No wonder it had overtaken them so easily, Carter thought; it was a low-slung, high-speed Porsche.

Speed was its undoing. It ran off the road, nose and headlights dipping as it plowed down a long, long embankment. A dust cloud marked its jouncing, shuddering descent.

"Punks!" Wooten crowed. "That takes care of them!"

Carter was doing some hard thinking. White Porsche —Prince Hasan—"an avid racing car enthusiast," Hawk had said.

Wooten followed the road in the opposite direction, rejoining the southern highway. They hadn't gone more than a mile when he said, "Uh-oh . . ."

"Something wrong?" Carter asked.

"I don't think that fancy maneuver was too good for the car. The wheel's pulling funny, over to one side. Feel it?"

"Umm." Carter pretended that he hadn't noticed Wooten surreptitiously feathering the brake pedal.

"Could be a bum tire," Wooten said with a show of concern. "I'd better pull over and take a look. We wouldn't want a blowout."

"Okay."

Slowing, Wooten left the road for its shoulder, coming to a halt in the middle of nowhere. No other cars were in sight.

Wooten sounded cheerful enough as he said. "I guess if there's a flat, yours truly is going to have to change it."

"That's why you're here."

"You're a hard man, Fletcher, but I like you."

The car stood on hard-packed earth. The boxy shapes and campfires of a small settlement showed far to the south. Carter and Wooten were the only living souls in this sprawling expanse.

They got out of the car. Wooten turned, a gun in his hand. "I got something for you, Fle—"

Wooten did a double take. Carter was not to be seen.

The Killmaster was hunkered down, using the car for cover. Wooten dropped into a combat crouch, trying to look everywhere at once.

Carter held the Luger under the car and shot Wooten in the ankle.

Wooten screamed, firing twice into empty air as he went down. Carter hopped onto the trunk, coming down on the other side where Wooten sprawled, cursing, agonized breath bubbling past clenched teeth.

Wooten was game, but before he could put his gun back into play, Carter stepped hard on the wrist of his gun-bearing hand, crushing it.

Centering Wilhelmina's snout on Wooten's forehead, Carter pried the gun from his fingers and pocketed it.

"You bastard!" Wooten groaned.

"Shhhh." Carter took nothing for granted and gave Wooten a fast but thorough frisking. The only thing it turned up in the way of weapons was a pocketknife, which Carter tossed into the darkness.

Frowning, Carter brushed off the dusty circles marring the knees of his trousers, from when he had knelt down out of sight. "Let's talk, Wooten."

Wooten's scream of obscenities was cut short by Carter's kicking his wounded leg.

"Suppose you save yourself a whole lot of unpleasantness and tell me who sent you," Carter said.

"Fuck you!"

"You want to be difficult? Fine." Holstering his Luger—Wooten was declawed—Carter went to the front of the car, tripping the button that unlocked the trunk. He went through it to see if he could turn up anything interesting that might persuade Wooten to be more forthcoming.

Jumper cables—jack—hunting rifle and a box of ammo—bottle of beer—bolt cutters—a toolbox—a can of powerful chrome-cleaning fluid. That would do it.

Carter grabbed Wooten by the collar and dragged him some paces from the car. Between groans, Wooten said, "Hey, what are you doing?"

Carter read the cleaning fluid's label by the trunk light. "Say, did you know that this stuff's highly flammable?"

"W-what? Hey, what are you doing? Don't—"

Sputtering, coughing, protecting his face with his hands, Wooten squirmed as Carter emptied the contents of the can on him, soaking him down. The stuff had a powerful alcohol smell.

"What are you doing, you maniac?"

"You've heard the expression, 'the heat is on'?" Carter said. "Well, buster, it's really going to be on you if you don't give with the answers."

"You wouldn't!"

"No? Watch me." Carter fished a pack of matches from his pocket and lit one. A sheltering ridge protected them from the wind, the small yellow flame burning steadily.

Carter flipped the match in Wooten's direction.

"Holy Christ, no!" Wooten squirmed away from where the match burned on the ground.

"Here, have another," Carter said, flipping some more his way. Wooten cried out each time a match fluttered near him. One missed his foot by a hair, his injured foot, and when he instinctively jerked it away, he screamed in pain.

"Don't, for the love of God!"

"I wonder if Howard Sale said that when they were working on him?" Carter mused.

"I don't know anything about that! I swear!"

"I'm not too fond of people who try to kill me, either."

"Wait!" Wooten panted, short of breath. "Wait. You've got it all wrong, Fletcher. I wasn't going to kill you. Just rough you up some, put you out of commission! I swear!"

"I'm not in the mood for fairy tales, Wooten." Carter set aside the matches and took out his cigarette lighter.

"Wait a minute! Give a guy a break, will you?"

"Howard Sale got a real break." Carter adjusted the wick to maximum aperture, so that when he flicked the lighter, it jetted a hissing twelve-inch tongue of yellow flame. "I don't want to set the world on fire. Just the part of it you're occupying, Wooten."

Wooten broke before the bright flame neared him. "I'll talk, I'll talk, for God's sake, stop!"

Carter flicked off the flame, keeping the lighter at the ready in case Wooten started waffling. Wooten made a pretty grim sight. Carter hated to see a grown man cry, though in this case he could live with it.

He fired questions at Wooten, not giving him the time to think up any lies. "Who're you working for?"

"You know."

"Say it."

"All right, I'm working for Hodler!"

"Now we're making progress," Carter said. "What did he tell you to do?"

"Get rid of you."

"Like you got rid of Sale?"

"I didn't have anything to do with that," Wooten said. "That was all Hodler's work. Sale was tight with the emir's people. He was snooping around, getting too close, sniffing around the club."

"The Crescent Club?" Carter said. "What goes on there?"

"That's Hodler's hangout. He's got it bad for one of the dolls there."

"A woman? Who?"

"A dancer. Sultana, she calls herself. He's nuts about her."

"You're lying," Carter said. "Hodler's not the type to let a woman get under his skin."

"This one did. Hey, what are you doing with that lighter? I swear, it's the truth! He's crazy mad in love with her—can't stay away from her. Even after Sale made him at the club, Hodler wouldn't lie low. He got rid of Sale instead."

"Who fingered Sale to him? You?"

"No. No! Hodler doesn't need anybody to tell him when he's being trailed. Sale was crazy to tackle an animal like that!"

"Not crazy. Just doing his job. All right," Carter said, "where do I find Hodler now? At the club?"

"No." Wooten shook his head until his teeth rattled, or maybe they were just chattering with fear. "Hodler took a trip out into the desert. He had to go meet the big boss."

"Who's that?"

"I don't know. Shit, you think he tells me anything? I'm just a stooge to him, that's all."

"That I can believe," Carter said. "What's Hodler planning?"

"I dunno."

"Too bad. You were doing so well up to now, too." Yellow-tongued flame whooshed out of the lighter.

It jogged Wooten's memory. "The Shiites! He's working with the Shiite radicals! They're going to off the emir and take over the oil fields!"

That made sense in light of what Carter knew about Al Khobaiq. Like his cousins the Saudis, Emir Bandar al Jalubi and his royal family were members of the Bedouin members of the Moslem Wahhabi sect. But the masses of the city were Shiites, the same sect as their radical Iranian cousins on the other side of the Gulf.

"What about Greer?" Carter asked. "Where does he fit in?"

"That asshole? He doesn't know which end is up. That's why Hodler wanted you offed. He was afraid that the Company had finally sent somebody who knew what he was doing."

"I want Hodler. Where is he?"

"I don't know, I swear it!" Wooten cried. "I don't know when he's coming back from meeting the big boss. They've got an airstrip somewhere out in the desert. That's all I know. Even if you burn me, I couldn't tell you any more."

"All right, I'll do that," Carter said. He made a few close passes with the flame, while Wooten writhed, sobbing, rolling on the ground.

If he wasn't telling the truth, he was giving an Academy Award performance.

The lights of the oncoming vehicle could be seen from a long, long way off in this wide flat space. Carter had plenty of time to get Wooten to the far side of the car, out of sight from the road.

"If these are some of your buddies, Wooten, the first bullet belongs to you," Carter snarled. "And just so you don't die too quickly, you'll get it in the belly."

The oncoming vehicle slowed as its lights picked out the limo. Carter stood holding Wilhelmina out of sight behind his back.

A rugged Land-Rover halted in front of him, driven by members of the Al Khobaiq Home Guard, a Bedouin unit presumably loyal to the throne.

Two soldiers jumped out, rifles at the ready, while a third opened the passenger side door for a young man in his early thirties with the air of command.

He was chunky, with a quizzical mouth half-hidden by a drooping mustache. His *ghutra* was silk, the head covering's expensive fabric denoting his royal status while contrasting with his custom-tailored European suit.

Carter recognized him from photos included by Hawk at the final briefing back in Beirut. He slipped his gun back in the holster.

"Prince Hasan, I presume?"

"Indeed, yes! And you must be the elusive Mr. Fletcher. Or, rather, Mr. Carter. It gives me great pleasure to make your acquaintance at last. I confess that when your driver ran us off the road, I feared we had seen the last of you. I was already composing my note of regret to your government."

Prince Hasan took in the miserable figure of Wooten, reeking of cleaning fluid, filthy, in pain, nursing his bullet-shattered ankle as he slumped dismally against the limo.

Prince Hasan grinned. "I see you have the situation well in hand."

ELEVEN

Every country has its share of architectural follies, and Al Khobaiq was no exception. A quarter-century ago, an eccentric member of the Jalubi royal family built a palace high on a hill overlooking scrub-covered eastern flatlands and the first rolling dunes of the western desert. The eccentric ended his days as a madman, screaming his lungs out in a padded cell. After passing through many owners, his white elephant of a palace now housed the Crescent Club.

Rumor had it that the palace was still owned by the royal family, who craved the pleasures it offered as much as any of their subjects. Leasing it to a syndicate of middlemen, they collected its revenues and partook of its delights while keeping their hands clean.

Certainly its owners had clout. A new road branched off the coastal highway, going inland for miles to connect with the mountain palace. The Crescent Club did a bang-up business. Carter saw more vehicular traffic on its access road than he had seen anywhere else in Al Khobaiq.

Ferrying the Killmaster to the club was Fawwaz, Prince Hasan's younger brother. Hasan's connections to the emir were too well known; a public figure reputed to head the secret police, Hasan's appearance might scare off Hodler from surfacing at the club.

Hasan was delighted to get his hands on Wooten. "So, here is the villain who wrecked my beautiful car!"

"Take good care of him," Carter said. "If my plan doesn't pan out, maybe we can use him as a lure to flush Hodler out from wherever he's holed up."

"Don't worry, I will take very good care of him," the prince promised. "I have just the place for this bad boy."

The prince's car had been wrecked, but not its two-way radio. Hasan had sent a message to Road Post 58, which dispatched a unit in the Land-Rover to pick him up. The unit then cruised the highway until they came upon Carter and Wooten.

After conferring on a plan of action with the Killmaster, Hasan and his men took Wooten to Road Post 58 while Fawwaz drove Carter to the club in the gray limo.

Surrounding the hilltop palace was an eight-foot-high concrete wall whose main gates were thrown wide open to accommodate the steady stream of long, luxurious automobiles delivering well-heeled, well-turned-out patrons to the club.

The sentries manning the gates were fierce-looking men, armed with rifles and daggers stuck in their belts. But security procedures were minimal, and Carter's car was waved through, into the central courtyard.

A circular drive allowed vehicles to drop their charges off at the club's main entrance. Many cars were parked off to one side, their drivers idling and smoking while waiting for their masters' return.

And so Nick Carter came to Al Khobaiq's gilded palace of sin.

The main building was a bizarre hybrid, cross-pollinating Moorish motifs with vintage Las Vegas glitz, garishly rendered in poured concrete, glass, and stressed steel. The fantastic creation had been built the hard way, with money squeezed out of the impoverished land prior to the discovery of the Zubeir oil dome.

Branching off on either side of the central structure were long, rectangular, two-story wings. Their ground floors were blank, windowless. The arched windows of the upper floors were barred by ornate wrought-iron grilles through which could occasionally be glimpsed the indistinct figures of the rooms' occupants.

These wings housed the so-called pleasure gardens, stocked with male and female slaves. Slavery is prohibited by man's law, but not by the Koran. Officially outlawed through the emirate, the age-old custom was still alive and flourishing.

Fawwaz's English was not as good as Carter's Arabic, but he managed to wish the Killmaster luck. Carter shook his hand, said good-bye, climbed out of the car, and watched the gray limo circle the drive and exit the grounds.

Eager patrons streamed across the plaza, under a portico, and into the palace. Carter joined them.

Inside, his nostrils detected a multiplicity of scents: roasting lamb, butter, spices, tobacco, incense, perfume, sweat. Noise racketed off the walls. Heat seethed.

The clientele was a mixed bag, fairly evenly divided between the Khobaiqi elite and affluent foreigners. The Crescent Club thrived—despite its flouting of Islamic and civil law—because the power structure wanted it that way. It looked as if a fair number of them were here tonight.

Carter prowled restlessly, integrating himself into the scene, getting a sense of it. As he always did when entering a place for the first time, he sought and memorized the location of exits, halls, and stairways. If trouble broke—when it broke—there would be no time to waste in searching for a way out.

Easing his way through the milling crowd in the grand front hall, he made his way to the main room, the club proper.

Some customs are universal. Slipping the attendant in charge of seating a handful of riyals bought Carter a table which, while not in a prime location, was as good as any allocated to a single fellow, as opposed to a big-spending party.

Carter surveyed the mingling of Middle Eastern and Western pleasure seekers. There were government officials, oil men, dealers and traders, buyers and sellers. Here sat a trio of Egyptians clad in conservative business suits, their heads crowned by red fezzes. There sat white-bearded sheiks from the interior, guarded by scowling desert tribesmen.

Female patrons were few and far between. Arabia was above all else a man's world. What few females there were, were European or American, sleekly expensive playthings plying their age-old trade in the emirate as the toys of powerful potentates. Carter wondered how many of them would conclude their Khobaiqi sojourn by being sold as slaves and shipped off to some sheik's harem in the great desert. More than a few, he decided.

Many of the patrons drank from porcelain teacups, but the crowd's roaring clamor suggested that they were fueled by something more high-octane than tea.

Raising his voice to be overheard by the waiter, Carter asked if it was possible to get a drink.

Indeed, it was possible. His whiskey was served to him in a teacup, outwardly observing the proprieties. It was watered-down, weak, and expensive, but it was authentic enough.

An intensive scan of the surroundings turned up no sign of Hodler. The towering East German would stand out in any crowd.

Carter faced front to watch the floor show. Big

speakers pumped in loud European disco-pop that had been popular ten years ago. But what the music lacked in interest was more than made up for by the live entertainment.

On the raised stage, a trio of girls writhed like flames in a high wind. They were voluptuous in the extreme, as their scanty costumes of sequined bras, G-strings, and filmy scarves revealed to the satisfaction of all concerned. Gold glitter dusted their sweating bodies, sparkling under the spotlights.

Spinning individually, the trio wove around each other in a kind of intricate belly-dancing minuet. Despite their near nudity, their faces were veiled below their come-hither eyes. Their caressing movements as they glidingly intertwined said that these lovelies were more than platonically fond of each other.

Heat, smoke, and noise filled the space. The dancers played to a most appreciative audience, who clapped and stomped and roared their approval.

As the music reached a crescendo, so did the action. These dancers had every part of their anatomy under control, with melon breasts, rounded bellies, taut thighs, and ripe buttocks all gyrating to the beat of a different drummer at the same time.

This was no striptease, though by the number's climax they had shed their glittering halters and all veils but the ones masking their faces. Heaving breasts sent dark nipples swirling in opposite directions, buttocks clenched and unclenched, heavy hips bumped and grinded, miming the thrusting movements of sex.

As the music peaked, the three graces shuddered, each flying high in her own individual orbit, paroxysming with orgasmic shudders as the sound suddenly ceased and the stage blacked out.

After a heartbeat's stunned pause, the walls shook as the spectators cried out in one many-throated voice.

The sweat beading Carter's face had nothing to do

with the temperature. That was some performance!

When the lights came back up on the stage, the dancers were gone. Carter noted that they had not been so carried away by simulated passion as to forget to collect the veils and garments they shed in the dance.

Waiters circulated, taking and dispensing orders. Carter stopped one of the fast-moving young men with a fistful of riyals.

The Killmaster surprised the waiter by speaking to him in Arabic. "When does Sultana dance?"

The waiter looked grieved. "Alas, Sultana dances no more. But there are many other fine performers who would delight in staging a private exhibition of their skills for a generous gentleman."

"No doubt, but my heart was set on Sultana."

"Alas, that is not possible."

Carter passed him more riyals, which rapidly vanished. "All things are possible for the right price."

The waiter shook his head. "Sultana's master is a most jealous man."

"Who might that fortunate fellow be?"

"A foreign devil of an unbeliever—begging your pardon, sir. But he is an evil man, a white-haired giant."

"Where does he keep this pearl beyond price?"

"There."

Ranged along both of the room's long walls flanking the stage were balconies subdivided into rows of private boxes whose intricate screens and sliding doors could be opened to watch the stage, or shut for more intimate pursuits.

The waiter's pointing finger indicated a box at stage left.

"Sultana is there?" Carter asked.

"Please accept this small token of my appreciation." Carter slipped some folded riyals into the waiter's breast pocket. His pleasure at the gratuity was offset by his dismay at Carter's recklessness. "Beware, stranger! Her master is absent, but he has set his dogs to guarding his property!"

"Dogs can be scattered by a few well-placed kicks."

"But these are evil men—killers!"

"Thank you again, you have been so very helpful." Carter glided past the waiter, who sadly shook his head at such rashness.

A steep flight of narrow wooden stairs rose to the gallery. Carter climbed them.

A turbaned guard stood behind a screen with brawny arms folded, blocking the entrance to the box holding Sultana and her two watchdogs. He stood half a head taller than Carter. His mean face was designed for scowling, while his muscular physique was built for violence.

"I have a message for Sultana," Carter said.

"I will see that she gets it."

"A message meant for her ears alone."

"Be gone, dog."

Carter tried the easy way first. "I have a message for you, too." He held out a handful of riyals.

Taking the bribe, the guard crumpled the bills and threw them to the floor. "Go away, little man."

Carter feinted, as if trying to slip past him. The guard grabbed a handful of Carter's shirt front, tearing it.

Carter draped his right hand over the guard's, as if patting it. Instead, he applied a claw hold that wedged the guard's fingers together in such a way that nerves were ground between the bones. An agonizing submission hold.

The guard was tough. He didn't scream, only vented a gasping groan. But he found it impossible to resist the Killmaster's punishing grip as his hand was twisted downward.

The guard's rolling eyes bulged as he dropped to his

knees. That put him in position for Carter's front snap
kick, which took him square in the belly. A hard, taut
belly, it was softened up by that kick.

Carter finished him off with a brutal, chopping strike
to the nerve junction behind the angle of his jaw. The
blow rocketed the guard off to slumberland.

Carter wasn't even breathing hard, though he did
break a bit of sweat while dragging the unconscious
guard off to one side, propping him against the wall.

Pausing to straighten his bow tie and tuck in his shirt,
he pushed back the sliding panel and entered the box,
closing the door behind him.

Sultana reclined on a divan, Arab fashion. Not even
the dark hooded garment wrapping her could disguise
the allure of her statuesque physique. Above the veil,
her eyes were almond-shaped, expressive, kohl-rimmed.
She looked dreadfully bored, until her languid glance
fastened on the figure of the Killmaster.

Her watchdogs' reaction was more animated.

Abdullah was burly, well muscled, with a graying
goatee. Missab was long, bony, and full-bearded. Both
sat drinking at an octagonal table.

Abdullah was the boss, or perhaps the only one of the
pair who spoke English. His frown at the interruption
deepened into a scowl at the sight of this brash Yankee
with his go-to-hell grin.

"What are you doing in here?" Abdullah demanded.

"I have a message for the lady."

Sultana looked nonplussed, or at least her eyes did,
all that Carter could see of her face. He liked what he
saw. He decided he'd like to see more of her, a whole lot
more.

First, though, there was the little matter of her guard-
ians to take care of.

Abdullah was obviously vexed. "How did you get
past the guard?" Raising his voice to carry outside the

box, he called, "Kizar! Kizar! Where is that fool?"

"I'm afraid your man is lying down on the job," Carter said.

Abdullah was the boss, all right. He threw Missab a dark, intent look of command, but Missab was already pushing back his chair to rise.

Carter swatted Missab with a blistering backfist that splashed his nose over half his face. The blow would have knocked him out of his chair, except that Carter caught him by the hair and yanked his head forward, slamming his face against the table edge.

The bottle on the table skittered, teetering on the edge. Carter let go of Missab. His hand was a blur of motion as it shot out, righting the bottle.

Missab, his crushed face a mask of blood, slid off his chair and dropped under the table.

Abdullah stood up, his hairy hand darting for his jacket pocket, reaching for a pistol. His draw never got started. His hand was still plunging into his pocket when Carter unleashed a front snap kick to the groin that mashed Abdullah's testicles to jelly.

Abdullah purpled. He took his hand out of his pocket, grabbed his crotch with both hands, and folded. He knelt on the floor, mouth gaping like a netted fish sucking for air.

Carter bent down, reached into Abdullah's pocket, and came up with a small pearl-handled pistol. He kept it, not wanting it, but only so he could dispose of it later. He used Abdullah's jacket to wipe his hand clear of Missab's hair oil.

Sultana's dark eyes were practically round. She stopped lounging, and sat up. Her veil billowed softly as she said, with no little admiration, "You are insane!"

He spoke to her in her own tongue. "We have a saying in my country: Faint heart ne'er won fair lady."

Carter thought he saw a smile under the veil. "You

think to win me, then?" she said.

"Not yet, but I'm working on it."

"You are amusing if nothing else, whoever you are. And just who are you?"

"A friend."

Wariness crept into her eyes. "All men want to be Sultana's friend."

Carter indicated Abdullah and Missab. "Those two weren't very friendly."

"They are no friends of mine." Dark suspicion clouded her face, as if she had smelled something rotten. "Is this a trick, then? Has *he* sent you, to test me?"

"Who?"

"My 'protector.' " She spat the word as if it were a vile oath.

"No." Carter smiled. "I said I had a message for you. Here it is. I have heard that you are very beautiful. I have come to see for myself. Not that I doubt the accounts of your beauty. But I wish to see it for myself."

He shot Sultana a burning look that left no doubt as to his intentions.

"Perhaps you shall," she said. "You may indeed be mad, stranger, but your looks are not at all unpleasant. I had begun to fear that all my admirers had been frightened off. But I warn you, you have made a powerful and dangerous enemy."

Carter shrugged. "What does it matter, as long as I have you for my friend?"

"That you have, stranger." Sultana rose. "Follow me, O rash one. I know a private place where our new-found friendship can blossom."

Missab was out cold. Abdullah remained where Carter had left him, crouched on the floor, clutching his crotch, hunched so far forward that his forehead brushed the carpet.

Sultana raised a delicate foot, pressed the sole of her

bejeweled slipper against Abdullah's shoulder, and pushed. He toppled over on his side, but otherwise remained motionless. It was all he could do to gasp for breath.

Sultana's laughter was scornful. Carter took her by the arm, escorting her out. At the threshold of the box, he paused to deliver his final message to Abdullah.

"Tell your boss that I'm taking his woman."

TWELVE

Sultana's status in the palace of sin was ambiguous.
She was no slave, although Hodler apparently thought
otherwise. She had free run of the place, and answered
to no one. As Carter followed her through the labyrin-
thine windings of marble halls and shadowy arcades,
they occasionally encountered guards. None of them
stopped or even challenged her, but respectfully de-
ferred to her instead. Carter guessed they were household guards, not Hodler's crew. He didn't know what
they made of him. Maybe they thought he was one of
Hodler's crew too. Or maybe they wanted no part of a
fight that wasn't theirs. It was clear that his leveling of
Abdullah, Missab, and Kizar hadn't provoked any
ground swell of opposition.

Carter had a difficult time keeping his internal com-
pass oriented among the maze of corridors and turnings, in obscure upper levels far removed from the
rowdy revelry of the club. Adding to his distraction was
Sultana herself, the nearness of her. She gave off an in-
toxicating scent compounded of perfumes, spices, and
her own musk.

The folds of her dark *chador* covered but did not conceal her womanly body. Sultana was blessed with the rounded, hour-glass figure that leaves fashion designers cold but puts men on fire.

They passed under a tower's arched portal, Sultana leading the way up a stone spiral staircase, through a second archway, down an L-shaped short hall. Halting before a door, she reached into the folds of her garment, pulled out a long tarnished brass key, unlocked a door, and beckoned Carter inside.

They were in an antechamber. Sleeping curled up on a floor mat, swatched and swaddled in black garments, was an incredibly ancient female.

Perhaps she was not sleeping, merely resting, for she sat up as soon as the chamber was entered. She was so old and wrinkled, she seemed a living mummy. Her chattering was animated and then some, her toothless mouth pouring out a torrent of what sounded like abuse when she saw Carter. Her dialect was obscure, and so fast, that Carter couldn't make heads nor tails of what she was saying. It seemed to be about him, and he doubted it was complimentary.

Sultana silenced her with a few short sentences, also spoken in that oddly accented dialect. Her words caused the crone to look at Carter with new eyes—no easy task, since her orbs were sunken in fleshy pouches and filmed with age. But there was disconcerting intelligence in her keen gaze.

"She is Faranyah, my slave," Sultana said. "She's a nuisance, but she's been with me for so long, I wouldn't know what to do without her."

She looked archly at the Killmaster. "I told her you have come to rescue me from my evil captor."

"She doesn't seem too impressed," Carter said.

"Faranyah said it would be a great and good thing if both you infidels killed each other. She is very devout."

Sultana shooed her slave away. Wailing piteously, the crone shuffled out the door, shaking her head and wringing her hands.

Sultana closed and bolted the outer door. She conducted Carter into her private quarters, beyond a beaded curtain covering an archway.

The inner lounge was sumptuous, in the Arabian manner. An intricate Persian carpet stretched from wall to wall. Long low divans were covered with cushions and brocaded pillows. Elaborately carved sandalwood screens and panels pleased the eyes and perfumed the air. Rich tapestried wall hangings adorned the walls in a riot of colored arabesques.

"What is your name?" Sultana asked.

"Nick."

"Neek."

"Close enough," said Carter with a smile. "Tell me, how did you come to be called Sultana?"

"That you shall soon discover for yourself."

Her hands busied themselves with the fastenings of her *chador*. It came undone, sliding off her curves to fall at her feet. Carter was dazzled by the splendor of her garments, and still more dazzled by the splendor of her body.

She was magnificent. Her wickedly ripe body was bedecked with jewelry. Jeweled rings glittered on her fingers, multiple strands of gold necklaces studded with precious stones and pearls fell across her heavy breasts. She wore a red-sequined halter top and a crystal-sequinned G-string. After a moment, Carter realized that what he had taken for red sequins were really rubies, while the G-string was set with diamonds.

"Are you as mighty on the field of love as you are on the field of battle?" Sultana teased.

Carter embraced her. She made quite an armful. Perfumed heat rose from her flesh, smoother than the gauziest silken veil.

He wanted her urgently, but he would take her slowly. Slowly . . . slowly . . . very slowly. That was best.

"Time to lift the veil," he said huskily.

He took off her face covering. She was perfection, her pouting lips an invitation. As her desire mounted from his caresses, she smelled sweeter still.

He found the catch to her halter, a maddeningly tricky clasp. It came undone and her heavy breasts tumbled free, her nipples like carnelian. He polished them with his tongue. Moaning, she stroked his hair, neck, shoulders.

She slipped free from his embrace, shedding her silks and beads and baubles in a dance that was old when Salome was young.

She moved away from him while he undressed, but not too far away. Naked and sleek, tawny flesh glowing in the lamplight, she sprawled on a chaise longue, a leg dangling over each side, her arms folded behind her head. It was as erotic an image as Carter had ever seen.

Looking up at his powerful, aroused body standing at the end of the chaise, she smiled and murmured, "Take me."

He plunged between her spread thighs and it took his breath away.

She was right. It didn't take Carter very long at all to learn how she had earned her name. She was a one-woman harem who made a man feel like a king. Or, in this case, a sultan.

Faranyah pounded on the outer door. Carter stood on the open-air balcony, looking down into the courtyard. It was still dark, but dawn was not too far distant, that hour when a good Moslem can distinguish the difference between a white thread and a black thread, and so knows that it is time for the morning call to prayer.

There was some kind of commotion at the main gate.

Carter was almost dressed. He adjusted the slings on his shoulder harness and holstered Wilhelmina. Now he was fully dressed.

Sultana threw on a robe and opened the door. Faranyah chattered at her. Sultana closed her eyes, then took a deep breath to steady herself. "*He* is here," she said.

"I know," Carter said.

He had Wilhelmina at his left side, Pierre in his crotch, and Hugo on his right arm. He was ready to raise merry hell. "Let's go," he told Sultana.

She was coming with him. He wasn't going to leave behind a ready-made victim for Reguiba's revenge.

Sultana picked up a leather pouch filled with her jewelry, the only item she was taking with her. A slight problem arose. She wanted to take Faranyah with her too.

"I can't leave her behind," she said.

But Faranyah didn't want to go. She shook her head while beating it with her palms, wailing her strong negative.

Sultana was worried and exasperated. "She does not want to go. She has not gone outside the compound walls for over ten years."

"You two work it out," Carter said. "I'll go down and greet our guest." He started for the door.

She halted him with a soft hand on his arm. "Neek."

"Yes?"

She kissed his cheek. "Allah be with you."

"Thanks. Be ready to go, once the shooting stops."

Carter left the suite. Faranyah and Sultana were still arguing over whether or not the slave would accompany them. A dark hush held the echoing halls of the palace. Its occupants would wait this clash out behind locked doors. Sultana had told him that the household guards would not get involved. Their only allegiance was to the palace of sin.

He went to meet Hodler.

Karl Kurt Hodler was an East German athletic prodigy. The state was his mother and father and it had shaped him into a scientifically engineered tool, first for athletic competition, later for destruction.

Hodler had gone to Munich in 1972 to compete for Olympic gold. He brought home a bronze medal, won in the grueling pentathlon. Today he would win neither gold nor bronze, but lead, the kind that comes out of the barrel of a 9mm Luger. He would, if the Killmaster had any luck in the matter. And Carter would need that luck, since Hodler was ranked as a world-class marksman with a pistol.

Hodler had brought back more than the bronze in '72. He had seen the work of the Palestinian Black September squad that massacred eleven Israeli athletes in the Olympic Village. That was for Hodler. He had finally discovered a team he wanted to join, namely, the league of world-class international terrorism. Since then, he'd won his varsity letter in sabotage and murder a hundred times over.

Technically he was still attached to the East German spy squad specializing in wet work, but in reality he was more or less a free agent, able to move around as he pleased, so long as his work coincided with Soviet-bloc goals. He hadn't been back home for over ten years.

Operation Ifrit wasn't a Soviet action. Militant Islam didn't need any direction from the Soviets, though they were glad to take all the Russian weapons and assistance they could get, as long as there were no strings attached. Since Ifrit's goals were the same as the Soviets— destabilization of hostile regimes in the Islamic world —the Russian bear was more than happy to lend a hand.

Hodler was an organizer and an expeditor par excellence. It's easy to motivate people when you're a killer. Two months ago he'd arrived in Al Khobaiq at

Reguiba's behest to take charge of the moving and shaking.

Hodler worked hard and played hard. On his first night in the emirate he had been taken to the Crescent Club by hosts determined to show their guest a good time.

Something unique in his experience happened to Hodler that night. He took one good look at the magnificent Sultana and fell for her hook, line, and sinker.

The icy East German death machine fell madly, obsessively in love with the Khobaiqi courtesan. He was addicted. He had to possess her utterly. No other man could have her, touch her, even look at her.

Initially, some of Sultana's admirers were inclined to dispute the point. One was found shot dead, the other had the larynx torn out of his throat by a killer who had broken the backs of two bodyguards to get to him. After that, the general attitude was that if Hodler wanted her that badly, he was welcome to her.

Sultana's wishes were of no importance in the matter. Hodler did not mistreat her, never so much as laid a finger on her in anger. And he was often angry at her coolness. She submitted in body but not in mind. His lavish gifts failed to impress her; his lovemaking left her cold.

No matter. Hodler was convinced that in time she would learn to love him. Especially since he saw to it that no other male got near her.

When he was away from her on frequent trips, he left three of his men behind to guard her. But last night, late, when he returned from fetching Reguiba and company in the desert, Hodler was confronted by three ruined wrecks named Abdullah, Kizar, and Missab. Learning that an unknown Yankee had leveled the three guards and moved in on Sultana, Karl Kurt Hodler went out of his mind with jealousy.

Searing him like vinegar on an open wound was the

image of Sultana, his woman, writhing in the ecstasy she had never shown him, offering all the charms of her perfect body to a stranger.

His pounding footfalls disturbed the birds nesting under the palace eaves. They made interrogative cooing chirps.

Hodler bounded up the front steps, under the portico.

A voice called his name: "Hodler!"

A man stepped out from behind a sheltering column. Hodler couldn't believe his eyes when he saw who it was.

"Solano?"

He'd met Solano, briefly, in Turin at one of Gianni Girotti's organizational meetings. The Italian struck him as brash, cocky, but absolutely capable.

Then last night Reguiba told him that Solano was in reality an AXE Killmaster named Nick Carter. Hodler had heard rumors about this American agent for years. And when he learned that it was Carter who had wrecked the Israeli action, he was enraged.

But he never in his wildest dreams suspected that the Yankee stranger who had taken his woman was Nick Carter himself. Until now. Now, he grasped the full dimensions of the big picture, and Karl Kurt Hodler just about went out of his mind. His fury knew no bounds.

All these thoughts spun in his reeling mind when he saw Carter. And that was too much thinking. For, while he was trying to sort things out to make sense of them, the Killmaster acted.

And shot the gun right out of Hodler's hand.

The impact broke Hodler's hand, even as the gun went flying. Hodler hardly noticed. He had gone totally berserk. Unarmed, he charged Carter's gun.

Carter had no intention of mixing it up with the six-foot-six-inch former boxing champion and power weightlifter. He shot Hodler in the left leg.

Hodler pitched forward, almost immediately scrambling up, lurching forward on one good leg, his huge hands outstretched to rend and tear. White foam bubbled from his mouth.

Carter shot him again, in the right kneecap.

Hodler went down again.

"That comes courtesy of Howard Sale," Carter spat.

Hodler was still in there pitching, fighting to drag his dead-legged body across the stones to get at Carter. Progress was turtle-slow, but he was game.

Carter shook his head, impressed despite himself. The East German giant's physical prowess was awesome. Hodler was like one of those indestructible characters in a bad stalk-and-slash movie. A bullet right between the eyes would stop him, but that was the last thing Carter wanted. Hodler had to be taken alive.

Hodler froze. Glancing over his shoulder, Carter saw the reason why. Sultana had emerged from within the palace, with Faranyah in tow.

For the first time, Hodler showed pain, anguish.

"Sultana—why?" he cried.

"Sultana is no man's slave," she said.

She started down the steps. "Stay clear of him," Carter warned, but she ignored him.

She stood over him, out of his reach.

"But I love you!" Hodler groaned.

"I hate you." From somewhere within the folds of her robe she drew a dagger, raising it high for the killing stroke. Hodler looked as if he would welcome it. But that was not to be.

The knife's downward arc aimed at the East German's broad, heaving back, but it never reached its target. There was a slapping sound as Sultana's wrist hit Carter's open hand, thwarting the blow.

"What are you doing?" she shrieked. "Let me kill him!"

"No." As gently as possible, Carter pried the dagger

loose from her fingers. At the same time, what felt like a bear trap closed on his leg.

Hodler grabbed Carter's ankle, trying to heave him off balance. Carter's free foot slammed Hodler's forehead with a stunning back-heel kick. Hodler let go, but he was still conscious.

Distraction was provided from a new quarter, courtesy of a throaty rumbling coming from the direction of the main gate.

A man, not one of the guards, pushed the heavy wooden door open, allowing an incredible auto to roll into the courtyard, around the fountain, and up to the front entrance.

Here was the "spaceship" car that Gus Ferguson had seen when Prince Hasan came to Petro Town to confer with Howard Sale. It was a Rotwang Plus-X, an exotic mid-engine, four-wheel-drive concept car, turbocharged and fuel-injected. The four-passenger, aerodynamically streamlined red auto's name translated as "Red Wing," but with its long snout and aggressive rear spoiler, it reminded Carter of nothing so much as a scarlet shark.

At a price of a cool quarter-million dollars, there were perhaps a dozen Red Wings extant in the world today. Here was one of them.

Prince Hasan hopped out. Pleasure smoothed the lines of fatigue in his face when he saw Hodler. "Nice work, Nick!"

"Thanks," Carter said. "You're right on time."

Hasan's face expressed even more pleasure when he caught sight of Sultana. "And who is your lovely and charming companion of this morning?"

"Sultana, meet Prince Hasan," Carter said.

"Delighted to meet you. Delighted!" the prince beamed.

Carter leaned over the semiconscious Hodler and

clipped him behind the ear with the Luger barrel, putting him out cold. Kneeling beside him, Carter pried open Hodler's lantern jaws.

Wedging two fingers in Hodler's mouth, Carter probed his back teeth. Sure enough, one of his back molars popped loose. Carter pulled it out.

"What on earth are you doing?" Prince Hasan said.

Carter held up the tooth. "It's a poison pill. All he had to do was bite down hard on it to get a nice mouthful of cyanide."

"We wouldn't want that! My uncle's staff of, er, interrogators, is looking forward to many a long and productive session with Comrade Hodler!"

"I'll bet." Carter knew that by "interrogators," the prince meant the emir's torturers. A Khobaiqi question-and-answer session usually began with hot branding irons and then got nasty.

Carter wiped his fingers clean on Hodler's shirt and tossed the tooth away.

Hasan was asking Sultana, "Did I mention that my uncle is Emir Bandar, my dear?"

"You can tell her in the car," Carter said. "She's coming with us."

"Wonderful!"

"Faranyah changed her mind," Sultana said. "She's coming too."

That didn't leave much room for Hodler. Carter and Hasan hefted the East German and crammed him into the trunk. Even with both of them carrying, Hodler was a heavy load. They had to get rid of an extra spare in order to fit him inside, and even then, it was tight.

Carter savored the irony. The East German liquidator would be making his last ride in a West German-made supercar. And it would be his last ride. Once he was delivered to the emir's dungeons, Hodler would leave it only to attend his own execution. According to Khobaiqi custom, he would walk to the headsman's chopping block. Although in Hodler's case, he would probably have to go via wheelchair.

It was obvious at a glance that it would be a tight fit, getting five in the Red Wing: Hasan, Carter, Sultana and her slave, and Hasan's younger brother Fawwaz, who was standing lookout at the gate, scanning the valley below.

"We can always steal a bigger car," Carter suggested.

"You might be able to steal a bigger car, my friend, but not a faster one," Hasan said.

The foursome climbed in the car, the females in back, Hasan at the wheel, Carter riding shotgun. The dashboard-mounted two-way radio crackled with static.

"I radioed Road Post Fifty-eight to send us some back-up," Hasan said. "Odd . . . they should have been here by now."

Fawwaz fired a burst into the air to attract their attention. He frantically waved his arms.

When the Red Wing paused at the gate to let Fawwaz climb in the back, they saw what had gotten him so excited. A trio of jet-black limousines rocketed up the mountain road, already a third of the way up.

Hasan said, "They're not mine."

"They're Hodler's," Carter said. "Let's get out of here!"

Fawwaz did not object to sitting in the back in such close proximity to Sultana, but he was taken aback by the stream of profanity launched his way by toothless Faranyah, abusing him for accidentally poking her with the butt stock of his automatic rifle.

Hasan tripped a catch under the dashboard, accessing a hidden compartment stocked with weapons and ammo.

"That's some option," Carter quipped as he selected a Swedish Carl Gustav M-45 submachine gun, slapping in its advanced rhomboidal thirty-six-round clip. There were plenty of spare clips on hand, too, as well as grenades and a sawed-off Remington shotgun.

The three black limos were more than halfway up the mountain when the Red Wing dropped down the road on the other side, descending the steep southern face.

Hasan handled the car like a pro on that wild roller-coaster ride, switchbacking through a series of hair-raising hairpin curves.

Carter looked back. Sultana sat bolt upright, eyes wide. Faranyah covered her eyes with her hands and moaned. Fawwaz grinned hugely. He was having a great time.

The last curve played out, dropping through foothills to reach a straightaway shooting across the plains.

A true motoring fanatic, Hasan shouted, "Now I'll show you what this car can really do, Nick!"

The press of acceleration pushed Carter deep into his seat as the Red Wing opened up, bulleting ahead. The horizon leaped forward, while the pursuers receded in the distance.

At that moment, the sun came up. Its angry red orb beamed long ruby rays across the desert landscape, touching it with fire. Jagged rock pinnacles and spires threw elongated shadows across the flatland.

Way, way back, the trio of pursuit cars crawled like three black bugs over the ribboned road.

Hasan laughed. "They'll never catch us now! We'll be at the post in ten minutes!"

Unease nagged Carter. "Didn't you say they were sending out some units?"

"Why, yes. We should have met them by now. I don't see them, do you? I'd better call again."

Activating his hand-held microphone, Hasan tried and failed to raise the outpost. Finally he made contact. Brief contact.

The post's radio operator was frantic. "We are under attack by a large force of heavily armed guerrillas! Repeat, we are under attack! We cannot hold them off much longer! Turn back, Prince Hasan. Repeat, turn back!''

And that was that. Following that message, the outpost ceased transmission, no longer responding to Hasan's urgent radio calls.

"Reguiba's on the move," Carter said.

"We'll have to turn east at the next junction and pick up the coastal highway! But there's no need for alarm." Hasan chuckled. "Nothing on the road can catch us!"

Nothing *on* the road.

The crossroads was empty of ambushers and everything else but highways and earth. The Red Wing slowed to 70 mph to take the left turn, its free-floating suspension showing no symptoms of stress. Safely set on the eastward course to the coast, the car once again increased speed.

Trouble arose out of the north, manifesting itself at first as a pinwheeling glare in the sky.

Nearness resolved the pinwheel into the rotors of a helicopter sweeping toward them on a swift, sure trajectory bound to intercept them in a matter of minutes.

Its shadow zoomed across the plains, overtaking the Red Wing. "Not one of ours," Prince Hasan said unhappily.

The copter was a lightweight, four-passenger job whose white fuselage was trimmed with green stripes. Not a military model, for which Carter was profoundly grateful, the chopper was a type favored by geologists making aerial surveys and the like. It had no heavy-caliber machine guns, and that was a break. But it did have gunners firing automatic rifles out of the ports and gaping side hatchway, slung back so the shooters could hang halfway out of it for a better firing position.

Air drag vacuum shook the Red Wing as the chopper overflew it. Its landing skids missed the car's roof by little more than six feet.

Executing a sweeping turn, the chopper came in for

another pass. The *whoop-whoop* of the whirlybird was counterpointed by stuttering automatic rifle fire.

The Red Wing caught the tail end of a burst, shuddering under the jackhammer pounding. Sultana screamed as the rear window exploded, cascading safety glass into the interior. She and Faranyah were huddled as low as they could get. Holes were punched in the trunk. Had the gas tank been hit, it would have been all over right there and then, but luckily none of the slugs tagged it.

Prince Hasan did some evasive driving, randomly cutting from lane to lane, slowing down and speeding up to throw off the gunners' aim.

Carter squirmed his upper body out the window. The airstream tore at him, seeking to rip the M-45 from his hands. He sat on top of the door, legs hooked tightly to keep him from toppling out.

Fawwaz joined the party, sticking the snout of his rifle out the window, pointing the barrel up.

The chopper overflew the road, coming in behind them. Carter's thighs already ached from the strain of wedging him in the window square, but he needed both hands for accurate shooting—as accurate as a submachine gun gets, anyway.

Twin spokes of fire converged on the rear of the car.

Hasan's evasive tactics threw off Carter's aim, but the Killmaster could hardly expect him to stop dodging. He could only wait for his chance, and when it came, he opened up with the M-45, squeezing off short sharp bursts. He targeted not the copter, but the gunners hanging out of its side.

He got one. The shooter dropped his weapon and fell forward, saving himself by holding on to the landing skid.

Temporary save. He couldn't hold on for more than a few seconds. His buddy was reaching for him, trying to haul him back inside, when the wounded man lost his grip and fell off the copter.

He bounced across an eighth of a mile of landscape before his tattered corpse rolled to a halt.

The relief that kill bought for the Red Wing was short-lived. The copter faced them, zooming low over the road, coming in for what looked like a collision course.

The dogfight turned into a game of chicken. Losing a man must have unnerved the other gunner, none of whose shots came close on this pass.

Carter's bullets ripped the copter's underside. He poured it on, going for the aircraft's gas tank. Landing skids came so close that he had to duck his head to keep it from being taken off. Fawwaz poured it on too.

The copter's roar was interrupted by irregular coughing.

The enemy wasn't so eager to rush in for another go now. They were in trouble. Tendrils of smoke wisped out of the copter assembly, thickening by the second into fat black snakes coiling around the craft.

Where there's smoke, there's fire. Once the burning began, it rapidly went out of control.

There was a *whoomp*, a crumping sound, then the first explosion—a small one. Pale yellow flame wreathed the machine's dragonfly body. The engine yammered, the copter yawed, pitched, shuddered.

The gunner tried to save himself by jumping. Had he been made of rubber, he might have survived the fall. As it was . . . .

The copter blew up, going nova, making the brutal desert sun pale by comparison. A mass of seething incandescence with a black helicopter silhouette at its heart.

The flying funeral pyre didn't stay airborne for very long. Leaning sideways, it plowed into the ground, producing a still more spectacular explosion.

End of copter.

Carter climbed back into his seat, his nerves starting

what would be a long, long process of untensing.

Fawwaz, delighted, fired off the rest of his clip into empty air to show his exultation.

"Everybody okay?" Carter asked.

No one was hurt, apart from a few minor scratches and bruises sustained by Sultana and Faranyah. The rear window was gone. A line of fat black holes dimpled the car's rear. The right side of the windshield was starred by a spidery impact web.

Prince Hasan breathed a heartfelt "Allah be praised!" at their narrow escape.

That did it for the opposition. The Red Wing reached Al Khobaiq without further incident.

The emir's crack units of Bedouin Home Guard were mobilized on full alert. Security was intense at secret police headquarters, where Prince Hasan rolled the Red Wing to a halt.

Those bullet holes perforating the trunk didn't look good for Karl Kurt Hodler. The lock was jammed and a burly guardsman had to jimmy the trunk lid open with a crowbar.

Hodler was curled up in a fetal position, steeped in a pool of his bright red blood. He was later found to have taken three slugs, any one of which would have killed him.

Sultana, hugging herself, asked, "Is he dead?"

"Incredibly dead," Carter said.

Karl Kurt Hodler had had the last laugh after all. He had cheated both AXE and the headsman's axe. A tough break, but Carter didn't seem as upset by it as the prince would have expected.

After a hurried consultation with an excited aide, Hasan was grim-faced. "More bad news. Road Post Fifty-eight was massacred, wiped out to the last man. That includes Wooten, whom I left there for safekeeping. He was gunned down in his cell."

The prince was sour. "What a waste! All that work, and we've lost both our leads, Wooten *and* Hodler. We'll have to start all over again, and—but you are smiling, my friend. What can you possibly find amusing about this setback?"

"We've got a source that's better than Wooten, and the next best thing to Hodler," Carter said.

"Who?"

"Sultana. The Crescent Club provided Hodler with a perfect cover. He used it to meet with leading subversive elements in Al Khobaiq. Pretending to be nothing more than pleasure seekers, the radicals met in the back rooms of the club to plot revolution with Hodler."

"Hodler is dead, Nick."

"Sultana is very much alive. Hodler was insanely jealous and possessive."

"I can see why," Hasan said, eyeing Sultana.

"He never let her out of his sight," Carter said. "Kept her with him at all times when he was at the club, even when he was busy plotting with his radical pals. Sultana knows them all, and will identify them. Once you put the arm on them, I'm betting it won't be long before one of them tips us to Reguiba's hideout."

"I see." Hasan nodded, smiling. As the implications sank in, his smile broadened. As the full effect of Sultana's curves hit him, he was all but beaming. "That's good. Very good!"

Carter grinned back. "I got some of the story from her last night, but I'm sure you'd like to talk to her yourself."

"Indeed I would! You will excuse me, please!"

Prince Hasan made a beeline for Sultana, and in no time, their two heads were together. Carter overheard Sultana asking him, "Tell me, are you really a prince?"

"Am I a prince? But of course! Emir Bandar is my father's brother! The emir regularly consults with me on security matters!"

Hasan took her arm. "But this is no place for a beauty like you, out here in the dust and the sun! Let's find a more congenial spot. We can drink mint tea and get to know one another better."

"That would be nice," Sultana said.

Off they went. Carter knew that Sultana was in good hands. Or was it the prince who was in good hands?

Catching the Killmaster's eye, Faranyah flashed him a nod, a wink, and a smile. Then she hurried off after her mistress.

THIRTEEN

Carter had Reguiba right where he wanted him, dead center in the cross hairs of his scoped target rifle. This was more of a firing squad than a military operation.

The Killmaster was not alone. With him were fifty members of the emir's Green Legion, the elite of the Bedouin Home Guard. Every member of this crack commando outfit was equipped with a rifle like Carter's, and qualified as a marksman.

They were the spearhead, the advance guard of this night attack. Nearby, waiting in the wings just out of sight, six companies of Home Guard infantry gathered, their firepower multiplied by machine gun-bearing jeeps and armored personnel carriers.

This was the cleanup.

Carter was right when he said that it wouldn't take long to get a line on Reguiba's whereabouts. Sultana arrived at secret police headquarters at midmorning. By noon, special squads prowled Al Khobaiq, collaring the conspirators she had named. It didn't take much squeezing to extract information from the plotters, not in a land where red-hot irons and the rack were standard police procedure. By early afternoon, the suspects were falling over themselves in their eagerness to confess everything they knew.

Emir Bandar was reportedly shocked at the extent of the conspiracy, which had enmeshed some of the city's leading families. He shouldn't have been. His royal family, the Jalubi, was a hereditary aristocracy maintaining a stranglehold on all the emirate's power centers. Many of the plotters were motivated not by revolutionary fervor, but by a desire to get a piece of the action.

But that was no concern of the Killmaster. Seen in the feudal context of Arabian politics, the emir was no better and no worse than the absolute monarchs of a dozen other kingdoms. Carter wasn't there to start a reform movement.

No matter what his faults were, the emir couldn't be as bad as what Reguiba had planned for Al Khobaiq.

The Zubeir Depression was a shallow bowl stretching some twenty miles. Under it lay one of the most extensive oil deposits in the world. Once the dome had been tapped and the wells came in, Al Khobaiq was awash in a sea of oil and money.

Acres of ground sprouted a forest of derricks. The area designated Field 89 was the scene of furtive, frantic activity as the Khobaiqi component of Operation Ifrit swung into high gear. Epicenter of the disturbance was a fenced-in compound as wide as a football field.

Dominating the space was an equipment shed as big as a dirigible hangar. Here was a motor pool and storehouse holding trucks, earth-moving machines, pipe-laying rigs, cranes, forklifts, and the like. It also held a fortune in smuggled weapons and explosives, which were now being passed along as quickly as possible to organizers of the insurrection.

The gigantic scale of the layout dwarfed the antlike streams of handlers and loaders moving the ornaments. A steady flow of diesel trucks entered the compound, pulling up to loading docks, stuffing themselves with weaponry. The matériel was earmarked for militant cells of Shiite revolutionaries among the rank and file oil workers.

The imposition of martial law in Al Khobaiq had caused the delivery timetable to be speeded up, but not fast enough. Time had run out. Zero hour was nigh.

The Home Guard was ready to crush the militants. They were prepared to sustain the loss of Field 89 in order to keep all the other fields. They clustered beyond the zone of light, ringing the compound, ready to move in hard the moment the signal was given. That moment was designated as zero hour.

But Emir Bandar was particularly concerned that the ringleaders be exterminated. To that end, a special squad of the Green Legion was sent into action, to infiltrate and to execute.

Carter was along for the party. As one of the few men alive who could identify Reguiba, his presence was vital. Plus, he would have hated to sit this one out. Reguiba's troops had done plenty of shooting at him, and it would be a positive pleasure to return the favor.

Like the members of the Green Legion, Carter was outfitted in camouflage-pattern combat fatigues, black jump boots, and a black beret. Like them, his face was carbon-blacked for added cover.

Two hours earlier, the unit began infiltrating enemy territory, taking great pains to avoid discovery. The complex mechanical environment of derricks, pumps, pipes, and storage tanks provided excellent cover.

Sentries and pickets were disposed of via the knife, the crossbow, and the garrote.

The commandos moved like ghostly shadows from one place of concealment to the next, closing in on the compound. Pumps and recirculators chugged away, drowning the sound of their approach. The compound was noisy with idling trucks, busy hoists, and the hectic pace of loading the weapons crates.

The vaulting equipment shed's twin slablike doors were swung wide open, its barnlike interior ablaze with light that spilled into the compound. It was the buzzing heart of this wasp's nest.

A railroad spur circled its solid real wall, curving around it and the rest of the compound. Loading docks fronted the tracks. Set atop the concrete platforms were long flat-roofed warehouses. They formed a high wall running the full length of the compound's northern perimeter.

Stationed in position, stretched prone atop the rectangular warehouse roof, were twenty-five Green Legion sharpshooters. Carter brought the count up to twenty-six.

The high roof provided a clear field of fire encompassing all the compound and most of the hangar's enormous interior. The marksmen had the subversives in a lethal shooting gallery.

The other half of the commando unit was deploying on the opposite, southern side. That area was a jumble of storage tanks and towers, supplying plenty of vantage points for snipers.

Carter estimated that the compound held about two hundred subversives. When zero hour began, they would be caught in a murderous crossfire.

Down there, forklifts ferried crates to the backs of trucks, where gangs of sweating men piled them in. Cocky gunmen paraded about, flaunting their weapons, disdaining the manual labor.

How soon before the dead sentries were discovered?

When would zero hour commence?

Carter peered through high nightscope, its high-intensity light-collecting lens turning night into gray phosphor twilight.

There was Reguiba!

There was no mistaking him. Carter could have

picked him out even without the special scope. His distinctive all-black clothes, lofty height, and arrogant stride were unmistakable.

Entourage in tow, Reguiba crossed the compound, entering the motor pool hangar. Carter felt as if he could sweat blood, he was so frustrated. If Reguiba went too deep into the hangar, he would unknowingly remove himself from the line of fire.

No. Reguiba paused at the threshold, engaged in some kind of confrontation with two other men who had hailed him and hurried to him. An argument, judging by the wild gestures made by the pair of newcomers. They looked as agitated as Reguiba was cool.

Prince Hasan consulted his watch, whispering, "Any second now . . ."

Carter made a minute adjustment on the sights, clarifying the target picture. Cross hairs centered on Reguiba's torso. Carter wouldn't even need to hit a vital organ to finish Reguiba. The rifle had such high velocity and penetrating power, that even tagging a limb would prove fatal to the target, swatting him down with massive pressure.

Ranged around Reguiba was his inner circle, a choice crew of misfits who held no interest for Carter. The head man was his target for tonight.

An excited character dashed into the compound, shouting and waving his arms. His words were inaudible, his alarm unmistakable. Unease stiffened the compound crew, who halted work to see what it was all about.

Somewhere in the tangled machinery bordering the compound's south perimeter, a flare gun fired a starburst shell. The missile climbed a parabolic arc, exploding in a hissing red fireball over the compound.

Zero hour was *now*.

Carter didn't even think about hitting the target. His concentration was far deeper than that. He *was* the target, identifying with it in almost a Zenlike state.

Letting out half his breath, utterly calm, he squeezed the trigger, firing the shot that would close out Reguiba's file in AXE's supercomputers.

Twenty-five rifles fired almost simultaneously with his, each sharpshooter taking out a different human target. It was doubled by a second crackling burst erupting from the rifles of the other half of the unit, opening fire from the south.

Total pandemonium broke out in the compound.

Prince Hasan targeted the driver of a truck that was idling at the front gate. The slug passed through the windshield and through the driver's chest. He bounced back off his seat and fell forward across the steering wheel, leaning on the horn, which blared nonstop, a brassy note among the percussive reports of the shooting.

Better yet, the truck now blocked the gate, obstructing that avenue of escape.

The flare's red light was the color that would do the least damage to the sharpshooters' night vision. Muzzle flares winked from roofs, towers, and other high points as marksmen picked off their targets.

A hailstorm of lead mowed down the radicals. They were in a blind panic, darting here and there, not knowing who or where to shoot, bewildered by all the bullets flying from what seemed like everywhere. Some fired their weapons off into empty air, merely to be doing something. Others who survived the initial onslaught dove for what little cover there was, huddling under trucks and behind crates.

Clamor in the east and west indicated that the Home Guard companies were on the move, charging hard. Powerful searchlights stabbed into the compound, throwing the scene of slaughter into high, harsh relief.

The militants spun, danced, whirled, died. No living thing could long survive the murderous fusillade. This

was no battle; it was a mass execution. A total rout. By
the time the Home Guard came on the scene, there
would be little for them to do but count the bodies.

Carter felt like hell.

Reguiba was still alive.

"He who pays the piper calls the tune."

Reguiba didn't see it that way. Not surprising, since
he was the piper in question. Sadegh Sassani and Nuri
Shamzeri did. They served as the eyes and ears of the
paymasters of Militant Islam. Needless to say, the difference of opinion generated plenty of friction in the
short time in which Reguiba had been saddled with the
young Iranian overseers.

Sassani was young, tough, pious, intolerant, unbending. Shamzeri, a Koranic scholar, was more intellectual
and philosophical, though no less unbending. A hundred times a day, ever since they had all come down to
Al Khobaiq on the same plane, Reguiba heartily wished
he were rid of the irritating pair.

The Supreme Council of Militant Islam sent Sadegh
Sassani and Nuri Shamzeri to see how their money was
being spent. Thus far, Operation Ifrit was less than a
howling success. The Al Khobaiq component of the action was of particular importance to the Iranians.

On paper, the plan sounded plausible. Those Saudi
puppets, the Jalubi, were a fractional minority dominating the Shiite masses thanks to their ferocious Bedouin
Home Guard. Arm the masses, raise the call to revolt,
and smash the emir and his royal family.

Sassani grudgingly admitted that Reguiba had established a pipeline for the vast quantities of weapons
bought from the Soviets by Militant Islam. Disguised as
pipes, drill bits, and other implements of the petroleum
trade, the crated weapons were off-loaded at the port,
then distributed by divers and sundry means to the
would-be rebels. A large quantity of them was sent via

railroad to the oil fields, to be used for the great uprising.

Sassani was skeptical. In truth, it seemed that his Khobaiqi brethren were less than eager for glorious martyrdom. Oh, they were more than willing to take as many weapons as they could get, but who wouldn't be? But as for using them to depose the emir and install a fundamentalist Koranic regime, they lacked that all-important holy fire, and seemed more than content to continue the status quo.

As for Reguiba, even a short time spent in his presence had convinced the Iranian that the man was godless and evil. This was suspected in Qom, but the Supreme Council argued that it was fitting to set him on the godless infidels and their lackeys. Sassani had not been so sure of the wisdom of that argument, and he was even less convinced now. Reguiba and his crew were devils. Devils!

Worse, they had failed to get results.

The action against the Zionists had been a disaster. Its failure was what had convinced the Supreme Council to send Sassani and Shamzeri to take a close look at how their money was being spent.

Sassani had not been to Egypt, and so he had no way to form an intelligent opinion on that action's chances of success. But even the short time he had spent in Al Khobaiq convinced him that serious problems afflicted this operation.

That was bad, since it was the Al Khobaiq mission that concerned the Iranians most. A number of divisions of Iranian "freedom fighters" stood ready to invade the emirate at the slightest sign of a popular uprising. Sassani had the uneasy feeling that the troops would be waiting a long, long time.

The hustle and bustle of activity in the compound failed to inspire him. He had a terrible vision of all those expensive weapons going into the hands of ambitious petty chiefs who would use them not in the cause of the Faith, but to carry on their own private wars.

Shamzeri shared these misgivings, and so the two Iranians determined to have a word with Reguiba on that score. Sassani suspected that the North African was turning a tidy personal profit on the arms distribution.

Sassani was an intense young man with wavy hair, a wiry body, and eyes like two black olives. Shamzeri was short, stocky, his eyes huge behind the thick lenses of wire-rimmed glasses.

Catching sight of Reguiba and his crew making their way toward the hangar, Sassani and Shamzeri intercepted them. Reguiba tried to brush them off, but the two were not so easily gotten rid of, as the man in black had already discovered to his irritation.

"Calm yourself," Reguiba said after listening to as much of the pair's complaints as he could stomach. The loss of Hodler had left him in a vile mood. "Your fears are groundless. All goes according to plan. Success is assured."

As usual, Mansour made with the flattery. "You dare to doubt the master, the perfect marvel of the age? Only Reguiba could have set so cunning a plan into control! He is the flaming sword of Islam!"

Carried away by his own rhetoric, Mansour stepped forward to press the point, sealing his own death.

For at that very instant, the Killmaster's finger tightened on the trigger of his high-powered rifle.

There was nothing wrong with Carter's aim; it was perfect. But the expansively gesturing Mansour chose that second to step in front of Reguiba.

Sassani heard a sound like a pickax thudding into a carcass of beef. It was the splat of the slug, taking Mansour square in the chest.

Mansour toppled backward, into Reguiba's arms. The crack of fifty rifles boomed out. The slaughter was on.

Reguiba saw the red crater gaping in Mansour's chest. His follower was dead weight, but still useful to the master. Reguiba used Mansour to shield him as he backed into the hangar. Lotah, Idir, and the Camel followed.

Sassani and Shamzeri didn't know what to do, so they ran into the hangar too. Outside, each passing heartbeat measured a further decimation of the ranks.

They ran deep into the building's interior, out of the line of fire for a moment.

"Success? Is that what you call this? You bungler! Fool!" Sassani shouted.

Reguiba wasted no time. He sought the way out. The far end of the hangar was a solid wall, unbroken by a door or even a window.

But standing in the hangar were some pieces of heavy equipment: a crane, a pipe-layer, a bulldozer.

The bulldozer!

Reguiba snapped out instructions to his men. Sassani and Shamzeri followed at his heels, shrieking abuse at him.

Idir and Lotah collected explosives and weapons, stacking them on the bulldozer. The Camel would drive; he'd once done forced labor on a road-building project during a term of confinement and knew heavy equipment tolerably well.

Auto theft he knew even better. True, the bulldozer was no auto, but the principle was the same. The Camel needed no key to start up the engine.

He pulled out some wires from the ignition, stripped their insulation, and touched the bare ends. Blue sparks sizzled.

Sassani said, "The great Reguiba—hah! The great blunderer! Is this, too, part of your cunning 'plan'?"

Reguiba seemed not to hear him. He looped bandoliers over his arms, dumped them on the bulldozer, then grabbed a half-dozen rifles and added them to the pile.

The Camel succeeded in hot-wiring the ignition. The mighty diesel engine sputtered, jerked, shook, then shuddered into life. Not even the torrent of gunfire could subdue the roar of the engine kicking over into full-bodied power, vibrating the concrete apron below its treads.

"What shall we do, Sadegh?" Shamzeri wailed. He seemed not to remember his oft-stated zeal to die for the Faith.

Reguiba and his aides clambered up on the bulldozer, huddling behind, around, and under its blocky projections.

Sassani grabbed Shamzeri by the arm, half dragging him over to the bulldozer. "Help us up!"

Suddenly the Iranians were looking down the bore of one of Reguiba's big .45s.

"Here's a message for your holy masters in Qom," Reguiba said. He shot down Sassani and Shamzeri, and then, for the first time that day, he smiled.

But there was no time to gloat. Slugs were zipping deep into the hangar, pinging off heavy equipment, punching holes in the walls.

A few militants who managed to keep their wits about them realized what Reguiba was doing, and tried to hitch a ride on the bulldozer. He shot them down too.

Obeying his master's instructions, the Camel threw the controls that lifted the machine's great curved blade so it was high enough to protect the riders in the open-top cab.

The Camel bounced around in the driver's bucket seat, throwing switches, yanking levers, engaging the gears, and opening the throttle. With a crushing grinding noise as the treads rolled over the concrete apron, the bulldozer jerked forward.

Idir and Lotah rigged a .50-caliber machine gun to

cover their rear. Lotah manned the gun, while Idir worked the ammo feed, keeping it from fouling or tangling.

The bulldozer chugged toward the hangar's rear wall, treads ponderously clanking, blade raised. Black smoke puffed from the stacks.

The blade battered the wall. The wall bulged outward, prefabricated panels popping loose from beams, corrugated sheet metal squealing like a thousand nails on a blackboard.

Vertical uprights snapped. The hangar rocked on its foundations. Somebody not on the bulldozer screamed that the roof was going to fall in on them.

The leading edge of the treads chewed up panels and beams. Night and space showed through a wrecked wall.

An instant of resistance, and then the bulldozer busted loose, plowing through the wall to the outside.

The somebody who screamed was right. The roof did fall in. Likewise, the rest of the hangar.

The slaughter fell off for a moment as the amazed sharpshooters watched the spectacle of the hangar collapsing.

Big as a tank, the bulldozer flattened a few fences and more than a few soldiers of the Home Guard who failed to get out of the way. A swath of destruction tracked its progress through Field 89.

A minute passed, then two.

Carter was not at all surprised by the tremendous explosion that lit up the sky. By now, he had a pretty good idea of the way Reguiba's mind worked. The man was a believer, all right. A believer in overkill.

The bulldozer had crashed into an oil derrick. The skeletal tower went over like a lamppost hit by a drunk driver.

A flashpoint of white incandescence was generated by the explosives that Reguiba and company had left on the machine shortly before jumping off it to safety.

The uncapped oil well caught fire. A line of brightness jetted up, up, up, rising to a hundred-foot-high pillar of flame. It cleaved the night sky with its intolerable brightness.

As a diversionary ploy allowing Reguiba and his crew to make their escape, the tactic was a roaring success.

Prince Hasan tried to console Carter. "I'll have an army turning over the countryside for him. He won't get far."

But of course, he did.

Which was why, a few days later, the Killmaster jetted to Cairo.

Reguiba was back in business.

FOURTEEN

Late one June night in the Cairo Museum, while
Major Fuad Akbar Namid of the State Security Bureau
was busy lecturing Nick Carter on the evils of Western
expropriation of Egyptian antiquities, the Killmaster
suddenly drew his gun and shot a mummy case.

Namid was nonplussed, to say the least. So was the
lovely lady professor whom he and Carter were protecting.

Namid was a big man in his middle forties. With his
imposing physique, gleaming bald head, and flowing
mustache, he resembled an old-time circus strong man.

An ardent nationalist and a staunch traditionalist,
Namid was not overjoyed at his assignment of being
nursemaid to an American spy and bodyguard to a
beautiful archaeologist. The spy belonged in Washing-
ton, and the lady belonged at home, tending a husband
and children.

By his standards, Professor Khamsina Assaf was well
on her way to becoming an old maid. Why, she was
thirty if she was a day, and still unmarried! And too
skinny for his taste.

Carter did not agree. Khamsina came from a fine old

Cairo family, and she was very attractive, though she did her best to hide that fact. She was also very intelligent, the holder of a doctorate and an important staff post in the museum, the author of over a dozen scholarly articles relating to her field, and was probably the world's leading authority on one of the Nile's most obscure tribes, the nomadic Nefrazi.

Her familiarity with the "Gray Raiders" of the desert was surprising, seeming more the province of an ethnologist than an archaeologist. But her antiquarian studies had taken her into the heart of Nefrazi territory, throwing her into prolonged and intimate contact with that fascinating people.

The turnings of fate, and the machinations of Reguiba, now rendered her knowledge invaluable. Information locked inside her head could unlock the secret of the Reguiba's final offensive.

She was tall, fine-featured, and high-bosomed. Her style was severe, almost prim. Her chestnut hair was pulled into a knot at the nape of her neck. Dark and lovely eyes were hidden behind owlish tortoise-shell glasses. She wore no makeup.

Her outfit consisted of a light brown jacket with a matching slim skirt. On this hot night, her navy blouse was worn buttoned to the collar. Slung over one shoulder was a square handbag. She carried a well-worn briefcase bulging with papers and notes relating to the Gray Raiders.

Carter had only arrived in Cairo a few hours earlier. By the time he had hooked up with Namid, his Egyptian counterpart, it was late indeed. The museum had been closed to the public for hours. By the time Carter and Namid arrived to escort her, even most of the dedicated staff had called it a night and gone home.

Namid had a car and driver waiting outside. When Khamsina was ready to go, the trio set off through the convoluted corridors of the museum.

They were on an upper floor of an obscure wing devoted to scholarly research. To conserve power, few lights were on, and those were sparsely scattered. A heavy smell of dust tickled the back of Namid's throat.

"Have you been to the museum before, Mr. Carter?" Khamsina asked. She seemed less interested in the answer to her question than she was in making polite conversation. The empty halls were quiet, hushed.

"Please call me Nick. Yes, I visit the museum every time I get a chance when I'm in town. It's endlessly fascinating. There's always something new to see. Or something old, I should say."

They passed a row of small, crowded offices, coming to a minor display hall, an intimate gallery. At its opposite end was the lighted landing of a marble stairway.

Earlier, Carter and the major had passed through this hall on their way to Khamsina's office. Then, lights shone in the gallery. Now the lights were extinguished, illumination provided by what light leaked in from the landing.

A broad aisle ran down the gallery's center. Rising on either side were glass display cases, their shelves filled with small items, such as mirrors, bowls, spice boxes, unguent jars, and other exotic bric-a-brac of the late New Kingdom.

Major Namid was a moderately religious man, when it did not interfere with his official duties or his pleasures. He knew that these rare antiquities dated from what Moslems call "the Time of Ignorance," prior to the coming of the Prophet, and therefore to be abhorred. By day, he would have been the first to scoff at any superstitious fancies, but there was something about the way the glass cases emerged from the gloom, separating themselves from the shadows, that he found a bit unsettling.

To take his mind off such thoughts, he paid more at-

tention to the conversation between Carter and Khamsina, to which he had been listening with half an ear.

He was pleased to note that the lady professor had ignored Carter's invitation to address him by his first
name. While he had no sexual interest in her—Allah
preserve him from educated women!—he disliked the
American flirting with a countrywoman of his.

Carter went on, "Yes, it's one of the great museums
of the world."

Irked, Namid said, "The collection would be even
more outstanding had not your Western colonialists
looted Egypt of so much of our priceless national heri-
tage."

Khamsina fretted at his bad manners, darting him
looks that he ignored.

They neared the landing, which lay beyond the
squared portal. Flanking the wide doorway were twin
sarcophagi, mummy cases braced vertically upright.
The mummies had long since been removed and were
stored in vacuum-sealed cases to protect them against
disintegrating from exposure to air and bacteria. One
case's lid was closed; the other was open to display its
interior.

Major Namid was riding his hobby horse: "I find it
somehow obscene that our two great obelisks are now in
New York City and London. It's high time your govern-
ments return the treasures looted from the Egyptian
people. You Westerners regard our country as little
more than your own private treasure trove . . ."

"Major, please!" Khamsina murmured. "Mr. Carter
is here to help us—"

"Here to protect his government's interests, you
mean."

"Which happen to coincide with your government's
interests," Carter pointed out.

"The time is past when you can take us for granted

and expect us to fawn all over you. Respect. You must respect a land that was civilized when your ancestors were living in caves—"

His hand a blur of motion, Carter drew Wilhelmina as he dropped into a combat crouch. No sooner had the pistol cleared its holster, than he pumped three shots square into the closed mummy case.

Khamsina and Namid were stunned. She spoke first. "Do you know what you've done? You've just ruined a priceless fifteen-hundred-year-old sarcophagus!"

Namid was utterly flabbergasted. He stood stock-still while the Killmaster padded on the landing, looking up and down the stairs.

Creaking sounded from the ventilated mummy case. That gave Namid even more of a jolt.

Namid's mind whirled, calculating how he could convince his superiors that there was nothing he could have done to forestall the American's act of insane vandalism. He jumped when the mummy case opened.

The lid moved, slowly at first, then faster, hinges softly squeaking. Suddenly the lid was flung open wide.

Inside the sarcophagus stood a man. Not a mummy, but a tall Arab, all long limbs and protruding knobby joints. He must have had a devil of a time fitting his long form into the case, Carter thought.

His dead hand still clutched a machine pistol. His chest was shattered by the Killmaster's three slugs. They were so closely spaced that the hole in his chest seemed one single wound. His shirt front was soaked a dark, glistening red.

He finished falling, tumbling free from the sarcophagus to slam facedown on the floor.

"What—how—who—" Major Namid sputtered.

"This is the one they call the Camel," Carter said. "He's one of Reguiba's top guns. Or, at least, he was."

"But—but how did you know he was in there?"

"When we came through here before, both cases were

open," Carter explained. "That put me on my guard when I saw it was closed. And when I saw the lid starting to move, I moved first. Of course"—he smiled—"if it had just been a practical joker, I guess I'd be in real trouble."

Khamsina was unsteady on her feet. Carter's free arm, the one not holding Wilhelmina, circled the professor's slim waist, steadying her.

"Are you all right?" he asked.

"Yes—no. I don't know," she said. "I don't care about him, but I'm so upset about the damage to the sarcophagus!"

Carter grunted. "I suggest we get a move on, Major. Reguiba doesn't do things by halves. There may be more like him."

Finally waking up, Namid pulled a snazzy Beretta, the little gun looking like a water pistol in his big hand.

"You are right—there may be more," he said. "I will go first to make sure the way is clear. You follow with the professor. We dare not risk her."

"All right," Carter said.

"I'll signal if all is well."

Before going down the stairs, Namid climbed up to the next floor, making sure no lurkers waited there. None did.

He was very upset. The joint mission was off to a terrible start. How could he have missed the detail of the closed mummy case? The agent was a smooth operator. A fast draw, too. The major had to get some of his own back, or suffer a serious loss of face. That was why he volunteered to pave the way.

He went back down the stairs, passing Carter and the professor. The American still had his arm around her waist. She looked distraught. Her head now rested on his shoulder, though she pulled it off when the major passed by.

The Yankee spy was a smooth operator, all right.

Major Namid's shoes slapped their soles on the treads of the stairs. He paused to step out of them. He had his gun in one hand, his shoes in the other. He went down the stairs in his stocking feet.

Another floor came into view, complete with landing, doorway, and darkened gallery beyond. He didn't like the look of it. Was that a furtive rustle of sound he heard, or was it only his imagination?

Nonsense. It was his proud boast that he was not an imaginative man. If he thought he heard something, then he had heard something. Listening hard at the top of the stairs for a moment, ears pitched to keenest alertness, he heard nothing.

He moved from the wall to the balustrade running along the stairwell, leaned over it, and tossed his shoes on the next flight below the landing, where they made a sudden clatter.

Two men ran out of the darkened hall, thinking to surprise him on the lower flight. They weren't his men, they had guns, and he didn't like the looks of them. That was all he needed to know.

One of them was trigger-happy and started shooting down the stairs before even looking to see what was there. His partner glimpsed Major Namid out of the corner of his eye, one instant before Namid drilled a hole right through that eye, into his brain.

The trigger-happy character had even less of a chance. Namid didn't wait for him to turn around, but punctuated his back with two snap shots along the spine.

The shooter lurched forward, hit the edge of the rail, folded, and dropped headfirst down the stairwell, making a hell of a racket. But he didn't yell, because he was dead when he went over.

Namid prowled the front of the dark gallery. It seemed empty, purged of all potential ambushers.

Further investigation failed to detect menace. He

called up the stairs, "You can come down now!"

Carter and Khamsina descended. The Killmaster was holding her hand. His other hand held Wilhelmina. His eyebrows lifted when he saw the corpse. "Nice shooting."

"The other one went over the rail," Namid said.

"Very nice."

Major Namid felt good. He had won his own back, restoring his lost face. It was, after all, quite unthinkable that he be bested by a foreigner here in his own bailiwick.

"The way is clear," he said. Already he was cooking up a cover story to explain the damaged mummy case. He could hang it on the Camel. That would head off trouble, eliminate paperwork, and satisfy his superiors in case the museum trustees made an issue of it.

They reached the parking lot without further incident.

Namid's driver, another Bureau man, sat behind the wheel, cigarette dangling from his lip as he read a tabloid by the car's dome light, totally oblivious of the gunplay that had gone down inside Egypt's most celebrated museum.

"Where have you been?" Namid demanded.

"Why—right here, sir."

"Didn't you hear anything?"

"No, sir. Did—did something happen?"

Namid could have cuffed his subordinate, but the presence of outsiders exercised an inhibiting effect.

FIFTEEN

Which was worse, the desert heat of Al Khobaiq on Arabia's east coast, or this inferno of Egypt's Western Desert, located just a hair south of the Tropic of Cancer? A moot point, thought Carter. As far as he was concerned, both sandy hells were equally unpleasant. At least in the emirate he was transported in long, luxurious, air-conditioned stretch limos. Here, 600 miles south of Cairo and 125 miles southwest of Aswan, he suffered and sweltered in a reconstructed mini-bus stocked with sweating soldiers, Major Namid of the State Security Bureau, Lieutenant Osmanli of the Army, and a Nefrazi brigand named Zarak.

Carter barely had enough energy to flirt with Khamsina.

"Is it true the Nefrazi are descended from a lost clan of New Kingdom Egyptians?" he asked.

"Where did you read that?"

"In one of your monographs," he said. "I have to admit, I'm no expert. I just skimmed the high points."

"Why don't you ask Zarak?" she said. "He's a Nefrazi."

Carter glanced at Zarak, scowling on the other side of the bus. "He doesn't seem too sociable. It's amazing that you get along with him so well."

"I told you, I was initiated into the tribe on my last field trip out here five years ago. The ceremony made me blood kin to all the tribe. To him, I am a sister."

Zarak looked like the kind of character who'd murder his own mother, but Carter kept the thought to himself. If ever a man looked born to be a brigand, Zarak did.

He knew Major Namid felt the same way about the Gray Raider. Namid came from a police background. Zarak was an outlaw. From the moment they had pulled strings to release Zarak from a Kalabsha jail, Namid and Zarak had taken an instant dislike to each other.

Khamsina said, "To answer your question, there are some strong suggestions that the tribe descends from the ancient, Pharaohnic Egyptians. Their name comes from the root word *nafr*, an old Arabic word that means 'hidden.' Much of their culture is virtually identical to that of the Bedouins, but the Bedouins themselves hold the Nefrazi to be idolators posing as good Moslems."

"They also call them the Gray Raiders."

"Yes, but that does not imply a judgment," she said. "All the tribes in this area, Bedouins and Nefrazi, have made their living by raiding towns and caravans."

The mini-bus was part of a military convoy going deep into Nefrazi territory, the tortured hills of the Sawda Hamadi, the Black Highlands, site of Egypt's newest and hottest brushfire war.

And Reguiba looked to be right in the thick of it.

Sadat had been a strong ruler, and paid the price for it. The current government in Egypt was well intentioned but weak. They had their hands full keeping the lid on the population pressure cooker that stocked the cities with legions of the poor, the sick, and the starving. They had recently been rocked by the Alexandria riots, and lacked the manpower and the firepower to mount a major effort to put down the troubles in the Sawda Hamadi.

It was popularly known as the war of the Gray

Raiders versus the Crime Police.

The Gray Raiders were the Nefrazi, strongest of all tribes in this, their traditional homeland. In the last few months, they had been hit hard by the Crime Police.

The Crime Police had actually been police not long ago, the underpaid, abused, infamous Riot Police who had rocked all Egypt by their rampage of looting and destruction in the tourist center of Giza not long ago.

The rioting Riot Police were quelled by the military, but many thousands of them had deserted, fleeing to the hinterlands. Most had scattered to the four winds, but a small army of them had gathered somewhere in the rugged lands of the Sawda Hamadi.

They survived and thrived by banditry, thievery, and raiding small villages. In this, they were little different from the native inhabitants, but their background combined with their nefarious activities had earned them the name Crime Police.

Starting at the time that Reguiba accepted the contract for Operation Ifrit, what had been little more than a nuisance had taken a quantum jump into a credible threat. The Crime Police were being organized and supplied with heavy weapons, forming a small, well-equipped, elusive guerrilla army.

Their first victims were the Nefrazi. They had taken a heavy toll of the various clans. The government could happily have wished a plague on both their houses, but the Crime Police had stepped up their actions to attacking military outposts and stations, wiping out the soldiers and looting the bases of weapons, gaining more recruits.

A fire fight in which the Crime Police got the worst of it had turned up some interesting personalities among the corpses. Some of them were Moroccan killers known to be associated with Reguiba.

Nick Carter's mission in conjunction with Major Namid was to establish friendly relations with the Nefrazi and, through them, seek out and destroy Reguiba and his Crime Police.

As hot as it was in the broiling mini-bus, Hawk was making things much hotter for the Killmaster. Hawk wanted Reguiba dead. Of course, Carter did, too, but Hawk wasn't letting him off the hook for Reguiba's getaway in Al Khobaiq.

Carter recalled his last conversation with AXE's chief before embarking on this trek west of the Nile.

"By the way, Nick," Hawk had said, "Griff and Stanton are operating in the area independently of your group. They might be able to come up with something if you're stymied."

That stung. But the Killmaster hadn't offered any alibis. He had had Reguiba in his sights and Reguiba got away. Actions speak louder than words. Reguiba, dead, would do all the talking for Carter.

Of course, the important thing was not to wind up dead yourself.

Professor Khamsina Assaf was known and trusted by the Nefrazi. That was where she came in. She was also concerned enough for their welfare to put her own skin on the line. Quite lovely skin it was, too, Carter thought, not for the first time.

Nimad, Carter, and Khamsina had flown down to Aswan, city of the mighty dam whose relative nearness to the Sawda worried Egyptian strategists. If the Crime Police ever grew strong enough to raid the dam, the consequences could be catastrophic, unthinkable.

From Aswan, they went south via hydrofoil to Kalabsha. That was where they picked up that charmer, Zarak.

Major Namid's sources informed him that a power among the Gray Raiders was sitting in a military jail for various crimes of violence. Khamsina suggested that freeing Zarak would incur a debt of honor on the part of the Nefrazi.

The local authorities vigorously protested the release, but Namid had the clout to make it happen. Zarak swore an oath on his sacred honor not to break parole, to aid and assist the searchers in negotiations with his kinsmen.

Carter and Namid both wondered what the word of a thief, outlaw, and probable killer was worth, but Khamsina argued that a Nefrazi would never violate his sacred oath, so they had to play ball. After all, she was the expert.

And so here they were, deep in Nefrazi territory, a wild land of wadis, sinks, sand, broiling plains, and a seemingly endless series of rugged gray-black ridges.

The convoy consisted of three jeeps and the mini-bus. The mini-bus was specially adapted to the primitive road conditions. It was fairly primitive itself, a rough ride, but at least it kept on going and didn't break down. It was equipped with a radio and a handful of hot, tired, well-armed soldiers who were so bushed that they didn't even bother to ogle Khamsina. Lieutenant Osmanli's threats to one or two of the more insolent wolves had nipped that in the bud.

A jeep rode in front of the mini-bus, a second brought up the rear, and the third ranged ahead as a scout. All three jeeps carried mounted machine guns. The scout jeep was equipped with a radio as well.

Extreme caution was exercised each time they approached tight gorges and blind curves. Soldiers went up on foot into the hills to search for potential ambushers. They hadn't come across any—yet.

Zarak, whose utter contempt for all things not Nefrazi was incredible, chuckled at the precautions. "All your men could not stop my people if they wished to destroy you."

Major Namid was too hot and tired to do more than make a disgusted face, but Carter was interested.

"How would they do that?" he asked.

"They would drop a mountain on you." Bored suddenly, Zarak went back to his pastime of snatching flies out of the air.

Khamsina explained. "It is an old Nefrazi trick, from the days when cavalry came to the Sawda to harass them. They would find a likely spot, at a mountain pass or gorge, undermine a section of the cliff face by driving long stakes into it, and pry the rocks off to crush their enemies."

"That gives us all something else to worry about. Beware of falling rocks, eh?" Carter said.

"Oh, they do not do that now. That was a long time ago."

"If it worked on cavalry, it should work on convoys too," Carter noted.

Presently they all had something else to worry about, and it wasn't falling rocks.

Station 6 did not reply.

Not a fort, hardly an outpost, Station 6 was the end of the line, the last stop before the road and semi-modern civilization ran out. It consisted of little more than a blockhouse, barracks to hold its complement of a dozen men, a well, and a gas pump. It would be the last stop, too, for Carter, Namid, and Khamsina before Zarak led them into the hills where the Nefrazi had their hidden oasis . . . and where the Crime Police base camp was secreted.

Station 6 had a radio, too, but they could not be raised by the operator working the set on the mini-bus. He was a youngster, fresh-faced, who said hopefully to Lieutenant Osmanli, "Maybe their radio is out of order, sir."

He didn't believe it, and neither did anybody else. The soldiers stopped looking bored and started paying plenty of attention to their rifles and ammunition.

The scout jeep went on ahead, out of sight of the rest

of the convoy, as they investigated the communications gap.

After a long pause, the scouts radioed back the reason for the unbroken silence of Station 6:

"They're all dead—wiped out!"

SIXTEEN

The vultures thronging Station 6 were having a great time, one of the best feast days ever. What looked like hundreds of them littered the ground around Station 6. They must have been there for some time. There wasn't much flesh remaining on the four clean-picked skeletons they were mobbing.

The real horror was in the mess hall. It was filled with vultures, too, smart ones who had figured out that walking inside the blockhouse would take them where the real action was.

Somebody had tried to burn down the station, but dried mud-brick doesn't burn too easily. Scorch marks framed square windows. Wooden doors, shutters, and roof beams were charred, blackened. The scent of burning was perfume compared to the indescribable stench within.

The mess hall was the scene of sudden, violent death. That's where most of the soldiers sprawled, amid the overturned tables and chairs. The sights, the stink, the blankets of flies . . . .

The men hadn't died by shooting, stabbing, or bludgeoning. Despite theirorted postures, there wasn't a

mark on them. Investigation of the kitchen told the tale.
Poison.

Still standing on a wooden table was the means of
death: a ten-gallon metal bucket with a long-handled
ladle resting in it. It contained *karkade*, a refreshing soft
drink made from raspberries. Its surface was coated
with thick black scum, the bodies of innumerable insects
who came to drink the poisoned sweet brew and, drinking, died. Just like the station personnel.

Carter told Major Namid the story that old Salah had
recounted to him on that faraway morning at SB headquarters in Tel Aviv, about the clan of Reguibat males
exterminated by a poisoned banquet.

Scanning the rugged black highlands, Carter said,
"He's here. Somewhere not far from here, we'll find
Reguiba."

Nothing is less romantic than a camel ride at night.
Some few miles west of Station 6, a bedraggled trading
post hung like a blister on the lip of the Sawda Hamadi.
Here mounts were acquired for the trek, one for each of
the travelers, plus two more as pack animals.

Major Namid gave final instructions to Lieutenant
Osmanli, charging him to establish a base camp, set up
his defenses, and maintain regular radio contact with
the town of Dunqul, keeping them apprised of the situation.

"And above all, maintan a constant watch over the
foodstuffs and the water supply," Namid cautioned.

Unnecessary advice, since the lieutenant had been
profoundly shocked by the atrocity at Station 6.

Osmanli was not happy with the situation. He trusted
Zarak not at all, Carter very little, and he was suspicious
of the woman too. But his orders were clear, and he
would obey them.

The little band waited until nightfall before setting
out on their journey. Not only because it was cooler,

though the sun's absence was a blessing, but because there was less chance of stumbling into a Crime Patrol ambush. Those renegades moved freely by day, but the night belonged to the Nefrazi.

This was not the first time the Killmaster had ridden a camel, but the experience was no more pleasant than the last time. His mount was surly, sullen, and balky, with all the maliciousness for which the so-called "ship of the desert" is famed.

Major Namid was reminded by his mount of another nasty trait of camels. They spit.

"Major, shhhhhh!" Khamsina said. "We will be heard all over the range if you do not control your temper!"

"My temper? Did you see what that brute did to me? He did it on purpose, I know it. Look at him, the devil's laughing at me!"

Carter noticed that Zarak, for the first time, was laughing too.

The Nefrazi bandit was enjoying himself hugely. They were in his world now, a world of harsh extremes and constant struggle.

Which described the Killmaster's world as well.

Carter had to agree with Namid. Even in the dull moonlight cast by a slivered crescent, the camel seemed to be giving the befouled Namid the horselaugh.

Once they were all mounted, they moved out on the trail in single file, Zarak in the lead. Hooves clip-clopped on the narrow, stony trails.

A rough ride got worse almost immediately, and Carter was reminded of yet another painful memory, namely, that camel saddles are damned uncomfortable. The camel's pitching, rolling gait rocked him from side to side in the saddle, soon making him wish he'd sewn a pillow to the seat of his pants.

The route passed through a gorge, across a stony flat, into a steeply rising, ever-narrowing wadi. Beyond the valley was a hill with a rounded dome, which they circled. The trek was no different from one taken a thousand years ago by the savage nomads who made this wasteland their own.

Within two hours they were deep in the Black Highlands. Zarak was in his element, and knew every inch of it, picking out trails no one else could find.

Carter oriented himself by moon and stars, but the trail took so many twists and turns that he was hard pressed to keep track of them. If he absolutely had to, he thought he could find his way back. He hoped he didn't have to.

Once, they saw a fire burning on a distant hilltop. It was extinguished almost as soon as they caught sight of it.

Occasionally Zarak paused, using all his senses, watching, listening, even sniffing the air as if to catch some elusive scent. At one passage he cautioned them to avoid making any betraying noises or talking. After twenty minutes they passed out of the tense danger zone.

By midnight the trail grew so rough that they all dismounted and led their camels by the bridles. Major Namid was careful to stay well clear of the beast's spitting range.

Eventually the ground leveled off and they remounted. They were on a sprawling plateau. For the first time in many a mile, there was the fresh scent of green growing things.

Zarak was true to his oath to lead them to the oasis of the Nefrazi. They arrived shortly after two o'clock, according to Carter's watch.

They entered a high-walled, narrow gorge. Overhanging ledges blocked the moonlight, locking the pass in inky darkness.

Was that an animal cry? Or someone imitating an animal?

There was a sense of movement, furtive, swift, all around them. Above them. But there was nothing to be seen.

The gorge widened, opening out into a bowl-shaped plateau hemmed in by cliffs. It was a vest-pocket oasis, dropped as if by mistake into the heart of stone. There was the smell of water. The bowl sported scrub grass, bushes, and small scraggly little trees.

At the left side of the bowl, the herd animals were hobbled, camels, sheep, and goats, sounding off with dull bleats, baas, and lowing.

And there were tents, ghostly gray, peaked, integrated into the landscape to take advantage of all possible cover. Clusters of them dotted the bowl, further camouflaged by the tiger-stripe pattern of moonlight and shadow.

"But where are the people?" Namid wondered.

Carter said, "They're here."

"No, it's deserted!"

There were no fires, no voices, and no one to be seen but the foursome, their mounts, and the distant grazing flocks.

But Carter knew better. He told Major Namid, "Take a good look around you. They're here."

"Yes, we are here." Zarak laughed. Not a pleasant laugh, but then he was not a pleasant fellow.

The Nefrazi appeared.

As if by magic, or mutual instinct, some common signal, figures erupted out of nowhere. Dozens of them, popping up like a few score jack-in-the-boxes, surrounding Carter and his party.

Tribal warriors, young and old. They all had rifles, and all of them were pointed at the intruders. Rifles bristled like quills on a porcupine.

Major Namid fidgeted as if he were thinking of making a play for his rifle.

"Don't," Carter said. "They've only got us outnumbered by about forty to one."

Namid confronted Zarak. "You tricked us! You led us into a trap!"

"I think not," Zarak said. "You seek the Nefrazi? Very well. Here are the Nefrazi. Some of us, at least."

Somebody in the crowd of riflemen recognized the voice, calling out, "Ho, Zarak, is that you?"

"None other."

This caused quite a stir in the crowd. The head man of the group came to the fore, his men respectfully making a wide berth for him.

He was a spry bearded elder, dignified, erect, with a face like the carved head of a walking stick, a long white billy-goat beard, and the eyes of a fanatic.

Malik, sheik of the tribe—for that's who he was—seized the bridle of Zarak's camel, while he turned his hooded gaze upon the rider.

After a pause, he announced to the tribe: "Zarak!"

They sent up a great cheer.

Sheik Malik asked, "How do you come to be here, Zarak? Did you break free from their stinking jail of stone?"

Zarak indicated Carter, Namid, and Khamsina. "They freed me. To them I owe my liberty, much as it galls me to admit it."

"Who are they?"

"I can tell you this: they are the enemies of our enemies."

"Then they are our friends!" Malik said.

"Perhaps."

"Thanks a lot, Zarak," Carter muttered.

Then Khamsina spoke up. "By the white hairs of your beard, O sheik, have you grown so old that you forget your little Khamsina?"

Malik recognized her, as did others in the tribe. The sheik commanded his followers to put aside their rifles. The trio dismounted.

The clan had gone through many changes in five years, but despite the losses caused by time and violence, many of Khamsina's old friends remained to welcome her back into the fold. They had not forgotten the city girl who had mastered their ways and been initiated as a blood sister of the Nefrazi. As her companions, Major Namid and Carter were made more than welcome, quite a change from a moment earlier. Carter's spirits soared once he was no longer looking at a hedgehog of rifle snouts. Automatic rifles, the ubiquitous AK-47. It was amazing how the Soviet weapon had penetrated into the most remote locales, he thought. But when there's a product that everybody wants, it gets around.

The more distant quarters of the oasis gave up their denizens, as the women and children emerged from their places of hiding to join the impromptu celebration. Not even the babes in arms had cried out until the all-clear was signaled.

Sheik Malik embraced first Carter, then Major Namid. "A thousand pardons!" he said. "You will forgive us for doubting you. We believed you to be more spies, like the ones we captured yesterday."

"Spies?" Carter said.

"Yes, come to ferret out our secrets! We trapped them in the wadi and netted them like hares!" He laughed triumphantly.

A heavyset, black-bearded man, the sheik's nephew, said, "I took this from one of them!"

He proudly displayed a pistol. It was a Walther PPK with a custom-made checked handgrip.

Carter had a sinking feeling in the pit of his stomach. The odds were against there being too many guns like that in these parts.

"Those spies—they're still alive?" he asked.

"Only until we plan a fitting end for them."

"They were rich with weapons and food. They enrich

us at their expense!" Sheik Malik said.

"I'd like to see them," Carter said. "It's very important."

"As you wish, so shall it be done, O honored guest of the Nefrazi! I will take you to them."

Carter and Major Namid followed the white-bearded sheik to a tiny tent set apart from all the others. Malik's nephew, Mugrin, lifted the flap.

Malik told Carter, "In light of the great service you have done us in returning our dear Zarak, I make you a gift of these two spies. Do with them what you will. Torture them, geld them, kill them, as it pleases you."

"I don't think that will be necessary," Carter said.

The two spies sat back to back, bound and gagged, tied hand and foot and to each other.

A twist of the wrist, a snap of the spring, and Hugo was in Carter's hand, thin and long as a knitting needle, glimmering in the moonlight. Hugo's dramatic appearance greatly impressed the sheik and his nephew. They came from a long line of throat-slitters with a real appreciation for knives.

Carter went into the tent and began to cut the prisoners' bonds. Over his shoulder he told the sheik, "Believe it or not, they're on our side."

"What? You amaze me!"

They were Griff and Stanton.

SEVENTEEN

This morning, the falcon was restless. It started violently at slight sounds. Its talons tore long slivers from the thorny branch where it perched, building a mound of wood shavings on the ground beneath it. Head bobbing, beak clicking, feathers ruffling, it communicated its unease.

Reguiba stroked its head, but the creature would not be easily soothed. Its close-packed feathers were as fine to the touch as fur.

"The helicopter is late," Idir said.

Reguiba shrugged. He was schooled in patience. All things came in their own time.

Presently, a lookout atop a rock cliff waved his arms. Idir said, "Here it comes!"

Water, camouflage, and weapons were the keys to the Crime Police camp. The camp was pitched at the site the Nefrazi called Ayn al Dra, the Spring of the Arms. Not long ago, it was a Nefrazi watering hole. Reguiba took it from them. Desert-born himself, he knew its value.

It was too bad that the tribesmen and his Crime Police were enemies, but how else could it be? There was not enough water for both. Somebody had to go to the wall.

The site was on the western side of a ridge, protected from creeping desert sands by twin rock spurs that curved far out, almost touching, forming a natural barrier. The spring itself was a bubbling pool of fresh, clear water sheltered by rock overhangs. A hundred feet above it was the hanging, house-sized boulder that some camp wit had named Nasser Rock because of its uncanny likeness to the profile of the late Egyptian leader. At the far end of the camp, directly opposite the spring, a flat stony oval served as a landing pad for the helicopters.

Covering nearly half the site was a complex network of tented tarpaulins, raised on poles and strung with lines, done up in camouflage patterns. It masked troops and supplies from the prying eyes of recon planes and spy satellites. It could shelter over three hundred Crime Police.

Reguiba enjoyed the thought that the onetime minions of the law were now his creatures. The desert and the Nefrazi had toughened them up. Soon they would be ready for big things.

He began the camp a long time ago as a project for the Libyans, who dearly wanted to destabilize Egypt. They had put him forward in Qom as the man who could lead Ifrit. They supplied his Crime Police with food and guns.

The troops were busy now, drilling, training, taking advantage of the short-lived morning coolness. Presently it would be too hot to move. Too hot for the *fellahin* city-dwellers, but not for Reguiba. He was a man of the desert.

The supply line was a long one. It began at Ayn al Ghazal, at the southeastern tip of Libya. Trucks ferried matériel across northern Sudan, by way of Selima Oasis, then over to Wadi Halfa. From there, it was

barged down the Nile to El Diwan. Libyan agents and
Egyptian traitors oversaw the last lap, bringing the supplies north by northwest in helicopters.

A fragile line. Without it, his Crime Police would
quickly wither up and blow away.

Diversions in camp were few. The helicopter's arrival
never failed to generate great interest.

The duo-rotor wide-bodied supply ship touched down
on the flat like a bee settling on a flower.

Noncoms formed up men to off-load the supplies.
The delivery crew didn't like to stay long. Reguiba was
mildly surprised when a half-dozen of them got out of
the copter and approached his tent.

They had guns. But why should that disturb him?
Everyone had guns. Perhaps a higher-up in the chain of
command was paying him a visit, and his men were trying to look sharp. Reguiba smirked at such foolish vanity.

The fellow in the middle of the group was familiar.
Where had he seen him before? By the time he recognized the newcomer, his guards had leveled their rifles at
the man in black.

Sadegh Sassani, the Iranian!

Sassani's left arm was in a cast and a sling. Come to
think of it, Reguiba did recall that he had fired a little
too far over to the left when he shot Sassani. He'd been
aiming for his heart, but Sassani must have moved.

Sassani savored his moment of triumph. "Yes, it's
me. No, don't move, not even a little. My men would
like to shoot you, so please don't give them the chance.

"It gives me supreme pleasure to put you under ar-
rest, Reguiba. You will be relieved of your command
and taken to Qom to answer for your treachery to the
Supreme Council, who will mete out the punishment
that seems fit. If I had the least doubt about their executing you, I would do the job myself, now."

Neither Lotah nor Idir were in sight. Trust those fools

to absent themselves the one time they were needed, thought Reguiba.

He said mildly, "What about the mission?"

"The mission will continue under the direction of Captain Wayyanid, here." Sassani indicated a glowering ramrod-straight individual standing at his side. "Captain, do your duty."

Wayyanid told his men, "Take that dog's guns and throw him in irons."

And then the helicopter blew up.

Taking in the forbidding desert scenery on all sides of him, Stanton said, "This is a hell of a place for a frogman!"

"You're liable to stay here if you didn't set those charges right," Carter said.

"They're right." If there was one thing Stanton knew, it was demolitions. He and Griff had trekked into the Sawda Hamadi with a pack train loaded with explosives. Their guides got greedy and tried to take it, so they had to die. But that left the two AXE agents lost in the wasteland. The Nefrazi found them, taking them by surprise. Those Gray Raiders had sneaked up on them in the middle of nowhere. They were good at what they did.

So was Andy Stanton. For the last two nights, under Carter's supervision, he and a team of Gray Raiders had skulked on the cliffs above Ayn al Dra, planting explosive charges in all the right places. It was a backbreaking, nerve-racking task, but it was done and the work was good.

When the radio-controlled master kill switch was hit, the charges would simultaneously detonate. The big bang would be something to see, but the immediate aftermath would be even better.

One of the toys he and Griff had carried in on the back of a camel was a medium-size mortar with incen-

diary shells, half napalm, half white phosphorus. Griff
was in place on a high spot now, ready to lay his lethal
eggs in the enemy camp.

When he and Griff had been taken by the Nefrazi,
Stanton was sure they'd get their throats cut at the drop
of a hat. They probably would have, too, except the
tribesmen were stumped by some of the fancy hardware
and wanted to keep them alive long enough to learn how
to use it.

Now they were all pals. The Gray Raiders were some
pretty great guys, in their own way. They sure had balls
aplenty. They could move and hide like ghosts.

Why, there must be over a hundred of them among
the horseshoe-shaped rocks around the Ayn al Dra. He
knew they were there, but unless he looked really hard,
they just seemed to be part of the landscape. A well-
armed part. After the big bang, they'd be there for the
mop-up. Should be a hell of a show.

Carter was hunkered down beside Stanton, cradling
the electronic detonating device known as the kill
switch. It was the Killmaster who'd come up with the
capper, and it was going to be a beaut. When he laid his
big plan on the Nefrazi, they loved it. It really appealed
to their pride of tradition.

It was very hot. Stanton took deep breaths and let
them out, but they didn't relieve any of the tension. He
was all keyed up.

Carter studied the kill switch. He'd never worked in
the field with Stanton before, but Griff vouched for the
kid, and that was recommendation enough. Still, he
couldn't help asking, "Are you sure everything's rigged
right?"

"Sure I'm sure."

"You're positive?"

"Aw, for chrissakes—"

"Never mind. Here." Carter handed him the kill
switch. "You can throw the switch."

"You mean it?"

"But not yet," Carter said. "Wait until I say go."

"Thanks. Thanks a lot."

"Have yourself a good time."

"When do I give it a go?" Andy asked.

"Wait until Major Namid takes out the copter," Carter said. "I want a clean sweep."

Major Namid finally worked himself into position. He had a grenade launcher, a satchel full of grenades, and a nice shady spot from which to shoot them.

The helicopter made a marvelous target, it was so fat and sassy. Time to fire the starting gun.

The launcher made a nice popping sound. The sound of the grenade hitting the copter was even nicer.

The blast blew the whirling rotors clean off, transforming them into flying guillotines that decapitated and dismembered twenty of the loading crew.

Sadegh Sassani, Captain Wayyanid, and the four rifle-toting guards had their backs turned to the copter when it blew up. There was no way that they wouldn't turn to see what had happened.

And they did. All but Sassani, who was caught up in a nightmare vision.

Sassani thought he was dead and in hell. The Moslem hell is a circular one, where the sinner is forever doomed to repeat his crime again and again for all eternity. He didn't look because he was frozen in place, knowing exactly what was going to happen next.

While Captain Wayyanid and his men were looking at the blast, Reguiba was looking for the main chance. He pulled his .45s and started blasting, cutting down the captain and his men before they realized they were being shot dead.

All except for Sassani. His arm was in a cast and he didn't have a gun and even if he did he couldn't draw it.

The last and only time he'd seen Reguiba smile, the man shot him.

Reguiba was smiling again.

He shot Sassani right between the eyes, and then he didn't have any eyes, and not much of the top of his head, either.

Griff had humped a mortar through the jungles and the rice paddies of Nam. He was a mortarman from way back, and it felt just like old times as he popped a shell down the tube and it jumped back out, right smack into the middle of three hundred stampeding Crime Police.

It blew up in a red and yellow fireball, spewing that good hot sizzling incinerating napalm. Even from high up in his perch, he felt the heat of it. He fired off some more and he had a nice roaring inferno going down there.

Hell, he'd fire off all the shells. It wasn't as if he'd get a bonus for bringing any back home. Besides, he was having too much fun.

Just like old times.

Except that this time, he was going for a win.

While all the fireworks were going off, Andy kept asking Carter, "Now?"

"Not yet," the Killmaster said.

Griff laid down a barrage at the place where a big gap opened between the two rock spurs. A sizzling, seething wall of hellfire now blocked off the main exit from the Ayn al Dra, boxing the Crime Police masses into a cul-de-sac.

They were scrambling like termites whose mound has been fired with burning gasoline, trying to get out by the sides. They ran smack into the deadly accurate rifle fire of the Nefrazi.

Reguiba wasn't panicked. He had found Lotah and

Idir and they were all sheltered at the pool of the spring, in a cool rock grotto at the base of the ridge. The hellish fire shells hadn't reached there, or even near there, though it was getting very warm. Any second now, they would make their break—

Now!

A long living shadow in fast motion, Reguiba darted out of the grotto, his men at his heels. Leaping from rock to rock, showing themselves briefly, using their heads instead of running into the fire or the meat grinder of Nefrazi fire—why, they just might get out of this alive!

The Killmaster told Stanton, "Give it the go."

Stanton pressed the kill switch. There was a horrible instant when nothing happened, and Stanton felt as if he was going to vomit.

Then suddenly all the explosive charges shaped around the boulders and overhangs of the ridge went off at once. Nasser's Rock bowed its hundred-ton head and dropped off the edge, an inexorable juggernaut pulping Crime Police by the score. Other charges loosened huge slabs of rock and dirt, a man-made avalanche that showed no mercy.

It was all over but the shouting, and the triumphant Nefrazi did plenty of that. As did Major Namid and the AXE agents.

Awed, Andy said, "What a way to go! Buried under a mountain of rock!"

Carter just grinned.

The dust hadn't quite settled when a shadow flitted over Nick Carter. He looked up to see what had cast it.

High up.

It was a falcon, a swift bird with a huge wingspan. It flapped between two mountain peaks and out of his sight.

An icy tingle touched his spine.

As abruptly as the mood had come, it went. Why, falcons were the least of his worries. His main concern was a hawk—David Hawk.

The head of AXE was going to hit the ceiling when Carter showed up late for debriefing, ten days from now. Ten days, during which he'd be enjoying a luxurious cruise down the Nile with the lovely Professor Khamsina Assaf.

And he was going to stick the tab for the trip on his expense account too.

DON'T MISS THE NEXT NEW
NICK CARTER SPY THRILLER

DEATH SQUAD

Carter went through first, with Morales right behind him. They ended up in a wide basin with the water bubbling over them and flowing out the other side.

As one, they rolled out of the basin and ran across a small courtyard to the safety of an overhang and receding wall. In less than a minute they had the oilskins off the AKs and the silenced handguns.

Above them they could hear the sound of the current watch's footsteps on the roof.

"The watch about to go on will be in the kitchen eating," Morales whispered. "The off-watch could be anywhere, sleeping, roaming . . ."

"We'll hit the kitchen first," Carter replied in a low voice.

They met number one before they got past the lower level. He was sitting on a ledge of the inner courtyard, smoking and looking out across the quiet valley.

Morales and Carter split and moved to each side, prone on the stones flanking him. Carter waited for a cloud to clear the sickle moon, and signaled for Morales to stay where he was. Then he crept soundlessly along the low wall and put a hammerlock on the unsuspecting guard from behind. At the same time, he brought Hugo into play.

The man started thrashing around, kicking and trying to shout, but Carter had a death grip on his trachea.

The stiletto went in and up between his third and fourth ribs, and the body went limp.

"Put him in here!" Morales rasped.

There was a heavily overgrown arbor hiding two love seats. They deposited the dead man on one of them.

"That's one," Carter growled. "Lead the way!"

They went through an alcove and down two flights of steps to the hacienda's lowest level.

"Kitchen," Morales whispered, pointing to his right.

"Wine cellar?"

"Down those steps," the old man replied, gesturing to the left.

They went right, and crept up to a slightly ajar door. There was a tiny window high in its center. Both men cautiously peered through.

Two men in fatigue trousers and green T-shirts sat chatting and sipping coffee.

"Use the Stechkins!" Carter whispered.

"Of course."

"I'll take the one on the right."

They crouched, and on eye contact rolled through the door. Both men fired from a one-knee position, emptying their clips to be positive.

"*Madre de Dios,*" Morales said, "a lot of blood."

"Too much," Carter agreed. "But there's nothing we can do about it. C'mon!"

They doused the kitchen lights and retraced their steps to the stairs leading down to the wine cellar. At the bottom, there was a tiny room with a table and two chairs. On the table was a lit oil lamp that threw eerie shadows off a steel-barred door.

There was no guard.

"Cover me!" Carter hissed.

Morales turned toward the stairs and brought up the AK as Carter moved to the door.

"Baldez . . . Ramón Baldez!" the Killmaster called.

A man emerged from the darkness between two cobweb-covered wine racks, and cautiously approached the gate. His bearded face was haggard and one side of it was covered with clotted blood. The white shirt and trousers he wore were tattered and filthy.

"Who is it?" he mumbled.

"Never mind who I am. We're getting you out of here."

"To kill me?"

"No, to make you the next president, I hope."

—From DEATH SQUAD
A New Nick Carter Spy Thriller
From Charter in March 1987

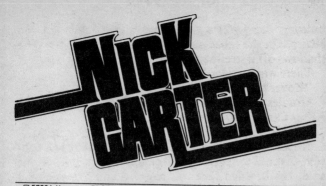

☐ 57291-X	BLOOD OF THE FALCON	$2.50
☐ 06790-5	BLOOD OF THE SCIMITAR	$2.50
☐ 57281-2	BLOOD ULTIMATUM	$2.50
☐ 06861-8	THE BLUE ICE AFFAIR	$2.50
☐ 57290-1	CROSSFIRE RED	$2.50
☐ 57282-0	THE CYCLOPS CONSPIRACY	$2.50
☐ 14222-2	DEATH HAND PLAY	$2.50
☐ 57286-3	DEATH ORBIT	$2.50
☐ 21877-6	THE EXECUTION EXCHANGE	$2.50
☐ 45520-4	THE KREMLIN KILL	$2.50
☐ 24089-5	LAST FLIGHT TO MOSCOW	$2.50
☐ 51353-0	THE MACAO MASSACRE	$2.50
☐ 57288-X	THE MASTER ASSASSIN	$2.50
☐ 52276-9	THE MAYAN CONNECTION	$2.50
☐ 52510-5	MERCENARY MOUNTAIN	$2.50
☐ 57502-1	NIGHT OF THE WARHEADS	$2.50
☐ 58612-0	THE NORMANDY CODE	$2.50
☐ 57289-8	OPERATION PETROGRAD	$2.50
☐ 69180-3	PURSUIT OF THE EAGLE	$2.50
☐ 57284-7	THE SAMURAI KILL	$2.50
☐ 74965-8	SAN JUAN INFERNO	$2.50
☐ 57287-1	SLAUGHTER DAY	$2.50
☐ 79831-4	THE TARLOV CIPHER	$2.50
☐ 57285-5	TERROR TIMES TWO	$2.50
☐ 57283-9	TUNNEL FOR TRAITORS	$2.50